The Malediction of Llewyn Glass

A Novel By

Frank Reteguiz

Amazon Edition

ataboolife@gmail.com

Copyright © 2018.

Cover by Lauren Renfrow

"Whoever fights monsters should see to it that in the process he does not become a monster." -Nietzsche

Prologue

Date: February 16th, 2015
To: Llewyn Glass, Esq
From: Sister Abigail LeFay - Vatican City, Rome
Subject: A Brief History of the Crossroads Pub

Situated in the Town of Fenway, which is on the outskirts of Boston close to the Charles River, The Crossroads Pub's location had an eerie history even before it was erected in 1723. Before Boston was colonized, the Massachusett tribe respected and feared the land where the Crossroads Pub would one day sit. Stories were passed down from generation to generation of the mysterious land and strange events which took place there. Tribal leaders would go there seeking wisdom during the day and come back with their black hair turned gray and their tanned skin turned ghostly white, with obtained knowledge so overwhelming that they could not repeat it. The tribes most honorable and bravest warriors would go hunting on this land and would return babbling uncontrollably of horrifying creatures which could only come from nightmares.

After the colonization of Boston, the land was left forgotten until 1692 when the Salem Witch Trials took place. Thirteen women of free thought fled south of Salem to escape the unjust and heinous persecution of witchcraft. They were only guilty of trying to enlighten themselves through curing ailments with herbs and expressing creativity through dance and chanting, but closeminded settlers had seen this as the work of the devil. The thirteen women fled to Boston for safety with a hunting party following suit when they came across the Massachusett's cursed land. The women, exhausted from their escape, rested on the

1

cursed ground and hoped to use the cover of night to conceal themselves from the hunting party, but despite the blackness of the night from the cycle of the new moon, the hunters found them. The thirteen women were flogged ruthlessly as the hunters repeated verses from the Bible in the hope of cleansing their souls.

After savagely beating the women, the hunters wrapped nooses around their necks and hung them from a tree with barely enough slack to stand on the tips of their toes. The hunters stacked kindling and bushels of wood at the women's feet while joking about burning witches for warmth. Twelve of the women begged and cried for their life. One was silent.

A hunter brought a torch close enough to her face to make her dried blood sizzle and pop from the heat, but she didn't move. She gazed stalwartly into the woods which slowly became darker and colder. One hunter slammed the butt of his rifle into her pelvis, but she continued staring back into the woods with a terrified expression before saying in an otherworldly voice, "I accept your offer." The torches of all the hunters simultaneously extinguished, leaving the woods pitch black and filled with bloodcurdling screams.

The morning sun soon came, and all thirteen women walked out of the woods, pale from fright and unable to utter a word from shock. The woods they left were littered with the detached limbs and ravaged torsos of the hunters. The trees were painted with their blood.

The thirteenth women who had accepted the silent, mysterious offer kept whispering to herself, "What have I done?"

In 1721, a Puritan named Jacob Martus and his family sailed to the New World to start a new life. He came across the same piece of land while hunting and was bewitched by the beauty of the forest. Jacob told his family that he felt an urge, a need to settle on the grounds. The family agreed and cleared the land and built their home and farm on top of it, not knowing the disturbing history of the woods. Jacob became a successful fur trader and saw the need to establish a pub so other fur traders could relax and conduct business before going into the wilderness to hunt for their pelts.

In 1723 the Pub was built and christened the Crossroads Pub for it was where fur traders, explorers, and other settlers would come as they were entering the wilderness or heading back to Boston. The family prospered and a small town was built around the Crossroads Pub with no unusual activity of any sort as until Fall of 1732.

It was a jovial night as the fur pelters were celebrating a good hunt with the local farmers who were celebrating a good crop. Everyone was drunk and merry except an old haggard woman who sat by herself weeping loudly. Mrs. Martus went to comfort her and asked her what was wrong. The only thing the woman said was, "I have to pay him back tonight." The Pub went silent over this strange statement. The woman slowly stood up and walked out the door into the woods.

Everyone watched from the windows as the old woman stopped and stood at the wood line a large dark figure appeared and loomed over her. The coldness of fright went through the spectator's spines as they watched the old woman talk with the terrifying figure. The conversation could not be heard, but the noise the creature made could only be described as bones cracking with a snake's hiss in the background. Suddenly there was silence and no movement from the two. The patrons and the Martus's watched in suspense as the world went still around the two. In an unholy act of mutilation, the creature tore the woman's torso from her legs and dragged the halves with it into the woods. The patrons collectively gasped, and some went into shock, but none of them spoke nor left the pub until the rays of the rising sun illuminated the empty woods.

The hunters and the militia went into the woods searching for the lady's corpse and the creature. They found only a plot of scorched earth a dozen yards from where the butchery happened. The bark of the trees surrounding the plot was burnt to a crisp with a putrid, rotting smell lingering in the air.

Whispers traveled throughout the colony of the uncanny event which brought forth the curious and the bold to hunt for the creature while the Martus's and those who witnessed the incident knew better than to trifle with the beast or the woods. Nothing more was found.

Years went by and the Crossroads Pub flourished from the travelers and the fur hunters. Jacob Martus died, and his son Samuel Martus took over the Crossroads Pub. The town grew larger and was named Fenway for it was close to the same-named swamp. There was prosperity and peace in the town of Fenway until 1776.

When the British took over Boston, many Bostonians took refuge in Fenway. With the rooms of the Crossroads Pub filled to the max, Samuel gladly fed and housed the refugees as the Colonial Army tried to take back Boston.

Fenway felt safe until the night of March 13th when a platoon of Redcoats rowed covertly up the Charles River and landed at Fenway. They were initially trying to land behind the Colonial Army in Boston, but they got lost and found Fenway. A firefight broke out, and Fenway's militia raged a fierce battle causing the retreat of the Redcoats but not before twenty bystanders and thirty-three militia members were killed in the process. Samuel Jacobs abhorred the brutality of war and wished to do right by the dead. He had the land outside the pub cleared and a cemetery was made where all of the bodies, even the fallen Redcoats, were buried.

It wasn't until 1779 that the Martus family started to notice strange occurrences in the cemetery. At first, they thought it was their drunken guests walking among the graves at night, but they began finding strange sets of tracks in the land and were hearing horrifying noises of creature's unknown. The Martus family and their guests would sometimes catch a glimpse of silhouettes of people moving through the woods and among the graves at night and found archaic symbols carved into the trees with the bones of animals set up as altars in the morning. This happened occasionally throughout the years, but nothing truly sinister happened until the year 1852.

Fenway had flourished into a small trading and fishing town while the citizens had grown accustomed, even amused by the ghost stories of their infamous pub/cemetery. At the time, the Crossroads Pub was secretly being used as a station on the Underground Railroad by Jabidah Martus. He was housing runaway slaves and ferrying them covertly across the Charles River. Jabidah and the Martus family were using hidden crevices in the pub to keep the runaways from being found and using the lore of the haunted grounds of the Crossroads Pub as a cover story for citizens seeing figures moving across the cemetery at night or unsettling noises coming from the walls of the pub. Jabidah was able to ferry hundreds of slaves and was able to do so without anyone in the town taking notice until the night of May 4th, 1852.

Jabidah was about to lead a small band of runaways to the ferry when they were ambushed by slave hunters in the cemetery. Not respecting laws nor life, the slave hunters beat the slaves and whipped Jabidah to the brink of death. They barricaded the doors to the pub with the Martus's inside and began lighting torches to set fire to the place. They wanted to send a message to the slaves and to whoever was helping them that death and misery would only follow.

Jabidah laid on the dirt helplessly as he was about to watch his family burn until he heard gut-wrenching screams coming from behind him. A loud thud sounded as something heavy landed close and rolled to the tombstone in front of him. Jabidah slowly looked up and saw the severed head of a slave hunter staring back at him. The head had been ripped from the jaw with its tongue hanging out. Jabidah went into shock and could not control his body, but he could hear the screams of the slaves yelling for whatever was in the graveyard to keep away as the slave hunters dropped their torches and fired their guns into the woods.

Jabidah could not move and kept staring into the eyes of the disembodied head lying in a pool of blood with its tail of torn flesh. He wanted to run but his body would not listen to him; he could only empty his bladder into the cold dirt. He heard screams of the slave hunters and the wet sound of their limbs being torn from their bodies as a rain of blood fell upon his back, but he still could not move... until something grabbed him.

He was hauled up onto his legs and dragged back to the pub by the slaves. They unbarricaded the door and ran inside. Jabidah managed to stand in front of the window as he watched the moonlight silhouetted figures of the Slave Hunters being torn to shreds by creatures he could not see in the dark. He tried to adjust his eyes, but a torn arm hit the window smearing the glass with blood, at which he fainted.

He awoke after being asleep for two days. The slaves had left in the early morning but not before burying the bodies of the hunters so the Underground

Railroad line would not close. Jabidah asked his wife what the runaways saw, and she said it was creatures not even hell could produce.

Years went by and then generations. Every once in awhile stories would circulate of strange things happening on the Crossroads Pub property, unexplained sightings of creatures, ghosts, and monsters, all dismissed as lore. During the early 1900s, people obsessed with the occult took trips to the Crossroads Pub with some leaving disappointed while others wishing they hadn't found what they were looking for.

Eventually, the eyewitness tales of the supernatural died down with the tales becoming urban legends while the Crossroads Pub itself slowly became a vacation and tourist destination as it was declared the Oldest Pub in America in 1999, and the longest family-owned business in 2014, having always been managed by a member of the Martus family. In 2004, an annual Halloween event at the pub became wildly successful as thousands flocked to the town of Fenway each year to take part in the celebration and the mystery of the Crossroads Pub. Everything was going well until the midnight hours of October 31st, 2015, when the myth will become a reality once again; because of you, Mr. Glass.

The Night of October 30th, 2015

The Crossroads Pub

Fenway, Massachusetts

I wasn't much for believing in scary stories about witches, monsters, or things that go bump in the night. My father, William Martus, would tell me the many legends of our family's famous property every night before bed. I would never believe him, even as a child, because I always believed in the rational. My father would laugh when I would try to find a way to explain what really happened without out the supernatural aspect of urban legends; he would then give a forced smile and tell me that I got my skepticism from my mother. She passed away from an aneurysm when I was 6. I don't remember much of her anymore, but what I do remember was the confusion of her being with me one moment and then gone forever in the next.

My father had a rough few years with drinking after my mom's death. It didn't help that he owned one of America's most beloved pubs, but he never let the drinking interfere with his role as a father or a business owner. If anything, he was a highly functional alcoholic, but I would sometimes hear him cry at the end of his drunken stupors for my mother. He would moan and curse God for taking the love of his wife away and cry himself asleep. But every morning he would clean himself up, hide his sorrow with a mask of a believable smile and get me ready for school.

He raised me the best he could by himself, but he often had help from the local patrons of the bar or his bartenders. I learned so much from the Pub; I learned how to gamble, how to make any cocktail in the world, and how to perform first aid from a few bar fights we had. Since my dad did not know how to take care of a daughter going through puberty, he had one of the bartenders, Missy-Jo, teach me about menstruation, make-up and how to be a young woman. Missy-Jo was an Irish-Puerto Rican from Tennessee who was fascinated with the lore of my family's property, and when she came to visit the Crossroads Pub, she fell in love with the Pub itself and hasn't left. Call it female intuition or, as she called it, "a bitch's itch" but I could tell she stayed for my dad.

Either out of pity or love, Missy-Jo always took care of him and helped run the Pub when his drinking became too much for him. My father gave her creative freedom with the Pub, and she was able to renovate it to its former glory. She started history tours during the day and ghost tours at night and created the Crossroads Pub Annual Halloween Festival. She brought beauty and love into our lives. I couldn't tell if Dad felt the same way, but he was at least just grateful to have her as a surrogate mother for me. I was glad she was able to fit the role for the few years she was with us.

When I was a senior in High School tragedy struck again. Missy-Jo was found dead in the woods outside the Pub. The police told the press that a bear attacked her, but it was a lie. They did not want to spook the town with the truth, but she was killed ritualistically. Her organs were ripped out and hung across the branches of the tree she was found under. Her eyes were missing, and she had strange claw marks on her body from an animal the police could never identify. I remembered the stories my father and his father would tell about the monsters and the evil that haunted our woods, and I started to believe they might be a bit of truth to them.

I cried for months for her, but it was my father who took it the hardest. He became overwhelmed with grief and took his drinking to a new level. One night he was found choking on his vomit in the Pub by one of the bartenders. He was rushed to the hospital, but he couldn't be resuscitated. Overcome by grief, I locked myself in my bedroom for days, unable to get out of bed or even eat; I lay there only wanting to sleep so I could not feel the pain anymore.

My uncle Ulysses reluctantly took over managing the Pub after my father died. He was always sweet to me and would tell me stories not only of the family's history with the Pub but of his adventures after escaping the family business. He was a well-known bar manager across the U.S. as he managed upscale bars and help them increase their profits. He loved the bar business, but he never wanted to manage the Crossroads Pub; as he stated, "the responsibility of bearing witness is too much." When I asked what he meant by that he told me that since the time our family settled on this mysterious and haunted land it seems whatever eerie or creepy occurrences happen here, our family's role was to bear witness to it. Then he would look into my eyes with heavy guilt and say, "You will be the first lady Martus to manage the business when you come of age, and you will have to bear witness; this is our family's curse."

Those words still strike a new chord every time I think of them. I tried to play coy in whatever Uncle Ulysses meant, but denial was a cheap facade whenever I went to visit the cemetery. I would sit in front of my father's grave, wondering to myself if the stories were true. Are we cursed to see unspeakable things and to what end? Why is my family cursed to this land of mystic and fear? Why must we witness the terrifying events? Why keep us at the Pub? I did not have the answers, but I resolved to get as far away from the Crossroads Pub as I could and not to let some twisted fate keep me on that land.

My Uncle Ulysses continued with Missy-Jo's ideas and was able to make the Pub the most profitable it has been since its creation by creating a micro-brewery which garnered national recognition. But, I was not content in staying so I snuck off after graduating high school and became a United States Marine; a title I loved dearly. I loved being in the Corps. I loved the pride, the adventure, and the new family I made within my unit; but I found out that my family curse cared not where I went, for it would always follow.

It was in my second year when my unit was deployed to Afghanistan to help train the new Afghan Army. We were a highly decorated Military Police unit selected to be an example to the liberated soldiers. It was a challenge I looked forward to, and I was excited to finally be deployed because I wouldn't have felt like I was a full Marine until I experienced war. I wished my naivety didn't lead me blindly into the horrifying event which destroyed my life.

It was the 31st of October 2014, and we were halfway through our deployment. We had completed training the Afghan soldiers, and now it was time for them to perform in the field. A squad of us accompanied a unit of Afghan soldiers to see how they performed and provide support for them. We were given a mission to a village 15 miles from the base to help them investigate a possible opium ring which was funding the Taliban. The sad thing was the beauty of the day; the weather wasn't too hot, and the desert landscape was beautiful to drive across once you forgot we were in a war zone. We came to the village and let the Afghan unit take charge as we followed behind. We scoured each house and found the town to be vacant, which was strange because our intel told us that the village was occupied.

The last house we searched was at the far end of the village. The overwhelming smell of death saturated the air as we approached it. I usually had a cautious feeling whenever we conducted a mission, but this one made my heart race. The Afghans kicked the door down and cleared the house halfway until they suddenly stopped with one of them turning around and vomited violently. The smell was so pungent; it smelt like I was walking into a slaughterhouse. I felt my boots stick to the floor as if I was stepping in puddles of syrup, but when I looked down, I saw the floor was flooded with blood. We made our way to where the Afghan's stopped and I saw what I couldn't possibly imagine war could have depicted. The entire house was filled with the butchered remains of the villagers. Their mangled corpses had their limbs torn from torsos and the bodies were positioned in repulsive sexual positions. I nearly cried when I saw children were also among the dead.

Before our Gunny could give an order, we were fired upon from outside. We took cover inside the house and went to the windows to see the enemy. There was a caravan of fighters speeding toward us.

When the Afghans saw this they immediately abandoned the house and cowardly ran away in the opposite direction. As if he wasn't surprised, the Gunny got on the radio and called for immediate support.

We had fifteen minutes to hold off the fighters, fifteen minutes in hell, so we did what Marines always do in an ambush; kill. We raised hell to the fighters and took out as many as we could, but they had the numbers and surrounded us. One by one my friends, my Marines, were gunned down until I, too, was shot in the leg and vest. I laid on the ground in agony next to the dying Gunny as blood gushed from his neck. I went to help him, but the gunfire suddenly stopped, and the multiple thuds of running feet came to our building. I looked into his eyes, and his last look wasn't of fear but out of grave concern. I was the only woman in the squad, and with the last ounces of life, he realized that raping and killing me was the very least these men were going to do once I was captured.

He took his pistol from his holster and aimed at my head as we both began to cry, and I gave a quick nod. He pulled the trigger, but the bullet didn't fire. He dropped the gun as he took his final breath. I cried for death to take me with him and spare me from the vile acts these men were going to do to me.

The stomping of boots stopped, gunfire erupted from all around us, and then it suddenly stopped. The front door was suddenly kicked open and the Marine support unit came rushing in; they had overtaken the caravan while I was on the floor. The Corpsmen checked on us and found only me still alive.

I was evacuated to the base and then to Germany to recover. I spent the days attending therapy and the nights screaming in my sleep. To my disgust, I had found out that the politicians back at home spun the truth to say that the Afghan soldiers were not cowards but had fought beside us and even helped protect me. The lie didn't make any sense, but I was given a stern warning by some General who visited me in therapy that I was to not disclose what happened for the sake of the war.

I didn't know what was more disgusting: the cowards who ran or the people who protected them, but I am sadly now one of the reluctant people who must protect the cowards and live with a lie. I could never look at the families of my Marines in the eyes because I knew that I told them a lie and if I told them the truth then I would find myself in Leavenworth.

I was medically discharged, and I came home to Crossroads Pub where Uncle Ulysses had remodeled my room and did his best to make me feel better, but I couldn't be reached. I reverted inside myself and did not leave my room for weeks. Uncle Ulysses was patient with me and did his best to help me heal from the trauma. He paid for therapy, got me a moped to get around town and called my old high school friends to keep me company, but I couldn't break out of my depression. Even when I started to leave my room and go back to working in the Pub, I would feel immense dread and hopelessness. I couldn't stop having flashbacks of the bodies and the Gunny attempting to mercy-kill me. I couldn't stop grieving and feeling guilty that I knew the truth but couldn't tell the families of my Marines.

Halloween was approaching, and I remembered the stories of the monsters my father would tell me as a kid. The terrifying creatures my father painted in my imagination were gentle compared to the horror's humanity can perform. Thoughts began to race in my head: "I don't think we should survive as a species because there is no good left. Where have the good men gone? Can we even save ourselves from our demise? Is there justice? Do we deserve to live on?"

The questions were repetitive, manic, and draining, all of which were answered with a sober but nihilistic answer: there is no good left in the world.

I decided on October 30th, nearly a year after witnessing the deep depth of the horrors of humanity, to bring myself peace and not live to see November 1st.

Crossroads Pub

October 30th, 2015, 11:57 pm

It was the night before the infamous Crossroads Pub Halloween party, and Uncle Ulysses had to go out of town for the night, so I was stuck watching over the Pub. Most of the tourist won't start partying until tomorrow night, so the Pub was filled with locals. Locals like our handsome Sheriff who unwinds his nerves by drinking a hot toddy and playing Texas Hold'em with the towns over-the-hill doctor, mayor, and mechanic. The Sheriff was always polite to me, and I knew he fancied me, as I fancied him, but I didn't want to hurt him. A couple of the local school teachers were here drinking and playing darts to calm their nerves for the upcoming week of dealing with their raspy students. Then there's the local ambulance chaser and Fenway's District Attorney sharing a meal together and making deals for their upcoming cases.

Everyone here are great folks to share the town with; they all knew about my battle and they did the best they could to show me some courtesy. But I could tell by their mannerisms that they didn't know how to talk to me. They beat around the bush and are overly polite when they see me outside on the few occasions I left my room, but they were respectful, which I appreciated.

Lenny, the Pub's brewmaster, was taking care of the final preparations for the Halloween Party while I was serving the patrons their drinks. I looked at the clock and every minute closer to midnight filled me with dread. I tried not to think about the bodies or the lie but the memories kept invading my consciousness, and I couldn't stop them. I put on a good poker face as I served the Sheriff his Hot

Toddy, but I wanted to go into my room and take all of my sleeping medication and fall into an endless, blissful sleep where there would be no more pain for me. I wanted to end the suffering. To end the panic attacks whenever I heard a loud noise. To stop rushing myself to bed so I could escape the burdening guilt to only have dreams of Gunny's last act on this planet an attempt to kill his friend mercifully. I wanted the pain to end desperately, and I didn't want to live a life tormented by those images and the burden of living with them.

The sound of thunder in the distance and the rapping of raindrops falling on the roof snapped me out of my morbid thoughts. I walked behind the bar to mix another martini when the front door flung open. We all looked toward the entrance as a gust of strong wind blew foliage across the bar floor. One of the teachers began to walk over to close the door but hesitated when she saw a dark figure walking from the parking lot to the front door. I didn't know why but at that moment my stomach turned upside down as I felt the dread of an unavoidable catastrophe approaching that I couldn't escape.

The figure emerged from the darkness dressed in a well-tailored black suit, a French-cuffed dress shirt with the top button unbuttoned with a loosened black tie; and a stoic demeanor underneath the smoke from his cigarette. The man grabbed the attention of everyone in the bar as he walked in and stood momentarily and looked around the bar scoping out the place. I stared at his face which looked like a young man who had aged fast from terrors untold, but the creases of the sides of his lips said he used to smile a lot. His hair was jet black but had sprinkles of gray.

He was ethnic from his tanned complexion, but I couldn't tell what his nationality was. I looked into his eyes briefly as he looked at the bar I stood behind, and I saw underneath his stoic face and his confident posture was fear, grief, and exhaustion; a man close to his end. But there was something about him that was off. I did not know what to make of it but there was a darkness that followed him. The door swung shut behind him by itself, spooking the teacher. The man walked slowly toward the vacant corner table as everyone watched in perplexity. He sat on the corner facing the bar and slid the ashtray close to him and put out his cigarette.

I walked over to him as he stared me down as if he knew me. "What can I get you, mister?"

He reached into the breast pocket of his suit and handed me $200. "Get me your most expensive bottle of bourbon and two glasses. Keep the change; I am going to be here for a while."

"Are you expecting someone?" I asked

"I have a date with the Devil."

He was all gloom when he said it but gave a smirk to lighten the mood. I smirked back at the minor lightheartedness he showed as I walked over and grabbed an unopened bottle of Pappy Van Winkle and two rock glasses. As I came back, he lit another cigarette and motioned for me to sit down. The dark sorrow he carried with him should of have scared me away, but his demeanor was hypnotic; he somehow made me feel at ease when he looked me in the eyes. I sat and poured the bourbon into the rock glasses. He grabbed one and pushed the other one toward me. He took a drag then a long sip of the bourbon, enjoying the taste of it.

He smiled at me and asked, "What's your name?"

"Lorelai Martus. What's yours?"

He took another drag of his cigarette and let the smoke and the question linger in the air. "Llewyn Glass. So, you're a member of the famous Martus family?"

"Yeah... next in line to run the place," I said trying to mask my dismay.

"Not only that but doesn't your family have a history... a myth of being around strange things, witnessing the unexplainable?"

"That's what the legend says."

"Good," Llewyn said with a little bit of glee. "Did you know that your last name is Greek?"

"No, I never gave it too much thought."

"It means to witness. And if the legends are right..." he took another swig of the bourbon, "then tonight you're going to add another story to your family's history."

"What are you talking about?" I bemusedly asked.

The sound of thunder grew louder as the raindrops began to barrage the roof. He took a long swig from his bourbon and looked me straight in the eyes with deadly seriousness.

"After tonight, you will tell your children how you met the Devil."

12:07 pm

I didn't know what to think at first. Was it a Halloween prank? Was he one of the sightseers who got too immersed with my family's history or is the man insane?

"Listen, Mister Glass. I know it's going to be Halloween soon and you're a fan of my family's history, but I don't appreciate having my leash pulled. I'm not in the mood for the stupid bullshit that you just tried to pull, especially tonight."

I got up to leave the table, but he gently grabbed my hand and stared at me with the eyes of a man who wants someone to believe him. Something inside of me told me to listen to him.

"I didn't mean to offend you or weird you out, but I need you to listen to my story, please," Llewyn said as he looked down at his hands as they began to shake. He no longer displayed the cool composure he had when he first walked into the room but acted like a man who was about to make his final confession.

"Ok, entertain me. Tell me your story."

The mischievous smirk came across his face again as he took a final drag of his cigarette before putting it out. "Thank you, but it's going to be a long one," he said as he refilled his glass.

The Pub's patrons pretended to go on with their business but listened in to Mr. Glass's story. I looked down at my glass and thought why not? Maybe I'll get one last good story before I take the final rest. I downed the rest of the bourbon in my glass and poured myself another. He began, "It started in 2012..."

The Fall of Llewyn Glass

Boston, Massachusetts. 2012.

I was once a Priest for the Holy Roman Catholic Church; something I wanted to be since I was a boy in Catholic School. I was attracted to the idea of being a figure of authority for God and saving souls and I was obsessed with the scriptures; the nuances, the interpretations, and mystery of them. As I grew of age, I joined a seminary and gave my vows to God; swearing to always serve Him, to deny the urges of the flesh and to live a virtuous life. My obsession with the scriptures as a child led me to my passion for the law in my later years. Fortunately, the Catholic Church pays for its servants of God to obtain higher education and they paid for my law degree and bar examination.

I was Father Llewyn Glass, Esquire., a title I was much proud of and often miss. I handled any legal cases the Cardinal would need me to manage in the Northeastern U.S., and I would do pro-bono work for the congregation to help serve the people I was supposed to be a Shepard to.

But that all changed with one confession. That horrible day when I sat in my confessional booth and a somber but guilty voice came from the other side of the screen and forever shattered my life.

"Forgive me, Father, for I have sinned. It has been three days since my last confession, but I have never confessed to this."

"Confess in peace, my son." I listened intently to his familiar voice.

"Father, I have served the church for all of my life for the sake of God, Jesus, and the Holy See. But I have..." the man took a deep breath as he held back his tears. "...I have partaken in sinful and illegal acts which I have grown physically disgusted with. I have done things that were horrible against the cloth, and I am sure that God won't ever forgive me."

"My son, there is no sin too great for Jesus to forgive. You only need to confess to it and let God come into your life to work it," I said with growing uncertainty. "Tell me, what weighs on your soul?"

"I've... I've..." he stopped for a moment and began to sob heavily. I slid the screen open to my confessional to hand the man a handkerchief and place a reassuring hand on his shoulder. The booth was quite dark at this time of day, so I could only make out a faint silhouette of the guilt-ridden man.

"I had sex with boys."

I reacted with disgust by yanking my hand off of his shoulder. But not wanting to ruin the confession, I placed my hand back on him and asked him to continue.

"I couldn't deny my strong urges. It first started out by just gazing at the altar boys at mass or when they came in to do their weekly tasks. I didn't think looking was wrong until the urges began to haunt my mind in all parts of the day. I denied the thoughts the best I could by praying and avoiding the altar boys and children when necessary, but the temptation became uncontrollable. In an act of desperation, I went to Bishop Kenny and confessed to him what was happening to me and how guilt was consuming me.

He calmly listened to me and put me at ease by confessing that he had to deal with the urges also. I asked how he overcame them, and his answer was my downfall, 'Sometimes to beat the devil you have to make a deal with him.' He smiled and told me to copy down the names and numbers he read out loud. After he was done, he said to call one of these numbers the next time I have those urges and the voice on the other line would help me out.

"It took me a month to work up the courage to dial one of the numbers on the list. When I finally did, a man with a thick Russian accent answered. I asked for a boy, and he told me to meet him in a rundown motel in Charlestown, to wear something inconspicuous and to bring $1k cash. I went to the motel, and I met with a large man with tattoos of nautical stars on his neck and fist. In a thick Russian accent, he asked me for the cash, and I gave it to him. He escorted me to a room and told me I had an hour.

"I walked into the hotel room, and to my sick delight, I found a preteen boy sitting on the bed. He looked peaceful but looking into his eyes I could tell he was drugged. But, I ignored all of my inhibitions and morals and let my temptation win in the hope it will finally leave me.

An hour went by, and it was both the vilest and most exhilarating moment in my life. It felt good to give in to my sin, to finally feel the passions of my flesh extolled. I laid there next to the boy, and for a moment I felt like I was in heaven. This was until I looked down and saw a tear run down his cheek. At that moment, I realized what I have done was wrong; this boy was suffering, and I didn't help him but added to it. Before I finished my thought, the Russian thug opened the door, not giving us time to dress and told me to hurry up, the hour was over.

"I left the motel disgusted with myself for what I did and not doing something to help that boy. I did what any other villain would do in that same situation, denied and blocked it from my mind. I found that to be easy and my temptations were satisfied for months until one day the urge came back full swing, and I couldn't help myself. I called a different number on the list and spoke to a boy directly on the phone. We met later that day in a dilapidated apartment where there was no Eastern European pimp but just a savvy 15-year-old who was in business for himself. Though he was young, life had made him mature for his age. I handed him the money, he took a hit of cocaine, and I gave in to my sin again. It was exhilarating and with less guilt this time; which made things worse.

"The time of satisfaction became shorter and shorter. I made a schedule of it and called the other boys on the list secretly while I still put on a front to my congregation and hypocritically told them to follow the word of God and condemned the sinners. But, each time I did it the guilt grew smaller, and the urge to do it grew larger until this past weekend when I couldn't live with myself.

"Bishop Kenny had invited me to a private party on Saturday for only a few elite members in the Boston area. He did not tell me what the party was for, but I accepted. I arrived in West Charlestown to a small mansion guarded by dangerous-looking men. I entered and was surprised to find some of the local Bishops and priests attending along with other men of influence outside the church: council members, local businessmen, and a congressman. I thought nothing about it at first as we were all talking business, politics, and small talk until Bishop Kenny called everyone into the ballroom. He thanked everyone for coming to the private gathering and said even though we came from different backgrounds we all shared one unique interest in common. At that moment, a door swung open, and a line of boys draped with white sheets came out and walked to the center of the ballroom.

"Bishop Kenny announced, 'Tonight we become free by giving in to our temptations,' as he yanked a white sheet off one the boys, displaying his frail, naked frame. Bishop Kenny grabbed the boy's genitals and forcefully kissed the boy, then proclaimed, 'Let sin rule for the night so we can live a life of decency.'

"I watched in horror as I recognized a few of the boys from the congregation, others as altar boys and one being the first boy I had my way with. They were manhandled and ravaged like meat eaten by savage vultures. The horrifying and grotesque orgy made me vomit whatever was left in my stomach as I realized I had truly lost my soul. I bolted out of the mansion, crying hysterically as I ran through the streets. I didn't go back to my apartment that night but wandered through the city looking for a way to forget. I got drunk at a bar and met a drug dealer who sold me some LSD which only intensified my guilt, disgust, and self-loathing with vivid hallucinations of Lucifer delightfully dangling my soul in his hands like a marble. When I became sober, I knew I must confess and try to make things right by talking to you, Father Glass."

It was half an hour since he began talking and I could feel my hand clench his shoulder and his shirt was now soaked from the sweat of my palm. I looked into the corner of the confessional and tried to remain composed against the tide of fury, confusion, and disgust, but it was of no use. I let go of his shoulder, ran out of my side of the confessional and yanked open the door to his side where I found Father O'Malley sitting there crying. I looked around quickly and found that we were alone, and I raised my fist and began violently beating him. I didn't stop until he held up an envelope covered with his blood. I stopped and grabbed it from him. Before I could ask what was in the envelope, he began to cry and stammer, and I gave him a moment to finish what he was saying before I continued to pummel him.

"Father Glass, you have a reputation of a man with unflinching integrity and you being a capable lawyer made you the ideal person to confess to. I didn't confess for God's forgiveness because I know he can't forgive what I have done, but I confessed to you in the hope you will do what it takes to make this right. The envelope has the names and numbers that Bishop Kenny provided me in that fateful meeting, along with the names of the men who were at the orgy, and my video recorded confession. I hope you do the right thing."

I stumbled backward and fell onto my ass on the floor. I just kept staring in shock at the envelope. I couldn't make myself move as I watched Father O'Malley calmly leave the confessional and walk out of the church. I sat there for hours into the evening until my cell phone buzzed with a text from the Massachusetts Archdiocese: Father O'Malley had committed suicide by jumping in front of a train. I stood up and walked to my law office a few blocks away from the church. Once I sat in my worn leather chair and felt safe again, I opened the envelope and found a list of names, numbers, dates, addresses, and an SD card of Father O'Malley's confession.

The next morning, I went to the Archdiocese for Massachusetts and presented him with the findings. There was silence between us as he looked over the evidence and watched the confession with a grave and exasperated expression. With his hands shaking as he held the file in his hand, he sat back in his chair and asked, "Are these the only copies you have?"

I hoped this wouldn't happen, and I prayed to God that it wouldn't, but that question confirmed to me that the Church was going to bury it. So, I lied. The Archdiocese petted my ego by telling me that I did a fantastic job and I did the right thing, and he was going to handle it.

But I knew what wasn't going to happen; they were going to transfer the

Bishop and the priests to other congregations across the planet and do their best to bury the crimes. And that was precisely what they did within a week after I presented the case. Bishop Kenny and the other priest were assigned to other congregations.

I had lost faith in my vows and the church. I was ready to sacrifice something I loved for something I knew was right, and I did it with two emails. The first email was my letter of resignation explaining why I was leaving the church and the events that led to it. The other email had scanned copies of the evidence and the uploaded confession attached to it and it was sent to the local newspapers, the Boston Police Department, and the Department of Justice.

It took an hour for the news to go worldwide. It took a day for the church to deny it. It took three days for the Church to perform damage control and quickly slandered my name in the press. It took seven days for uproars from the public and the pundits to rebel against the church. Within 40 days, some of the clergymen, businessmen, and politicians involved in the pedophile ring were arrested while the most powerful ones used their influence, power, and money to get out of it; including Bishop Kenny who got a cushy position in Switzerland which happens to be non-extraditable.

The Holy See didn't attack me by demanding me to pay back the tuition for my law degree nor did they excommunicate me, but they made it hard for me to begin a new life. I was able to start my new firm, but I had to start defending people I knew were guilty to make ends meet. It didn't take two months for me to regret me doing the right thing as I had to swallow my integrity and character and tell the courts that my guilty clients were innocent so that I can eat. I lost my faith in God and the idea of justice.

I had a glimpse of hope when a new client walked in. Her name was Lilith. Her skin was milky white, her frame was slender but had curves in the right places, and she had raven black hair with curls which complimented her blue eyes. She came into my office because she was charged with arson and public intoxication in a public park for performing what she said was a "religious ceremony" and needed counsel. She admitted to eating magic mushrooms and performing a pagan ritual from a hobby of studying mythology. Despite her eccentricity, I couldn't help to be mesmerized by her presence.

Of course, while I was a priest I had urges for the flesh and wanted to bed a woman, but I never entertained or acted on them, even after leaving the church. I was too distraught and heartbroken from losing my faith to even think about dating, but meeting her made me forget the sadness and loss; she made me feel human. We talked for hours in my office, and I began to fall in love for the first time in 30 years. That night we went out for dinner and we shared a sweet kiss; a first for me. I had never expected in my life to feel the intensity of love for another person. I defended Lilith's case within the week and got her off with community service. The night after winning her case we made love for the first time. Never have I ever felt anything so exhilarating or fantastic than having sex for the first time; it made me regret being celibate for all my life.

I felt I could finally move on with my life. We were inseparable for months as I bathed in the joys of being in love. She would stay with me in my apartment every night and go to the museum in the mornings for her job as a historian. Lilith rarely talked about her family, she just told me that she was adopted at birth and never met her birth-parents nor sought them out. She was a bit of an eccentric due to her obsession with mythology and American colonial history, but I found it endearing. Lilith would smile with her eyes and her dimples made me tremble each time I saw them. The best thing she did for me was to listen to my hurt when I told her what happened to me with the church, the disgust I felt for them not doing the right thing, and how I felt like what I did wasn't enough. Lilith would always listen and comfort me. Two months into dating I bought a ring to propose. I was on top of the world and felt like I was given a gift from life until I got home, and she gave me the tragic news. Lilith had lung cancer, and it was highly aggressive.

She went to the doctor for complaints of chest pain and left with an x-ray showing most of her lungs covered in tumors. She didn't have long to live. Chemo and radiation therapy were useless at this point, and the doctor just advised her to settle her affairs and make the best of the time she had left. We cried in each other's arms for hours that night. When she finally fell asleep, I went for a walk to the bodega down the street and bought my first pack of cigarettes. I coughed hard as I inhaled the hot smoke; it forced me to tear up and then I lost control of my emotions and fell to my knees and cursed at God. "How fucking dare you! After what I did and went through this is how you treat me! You asshole! You amoral omnipresent dick! Why her? Why do this to me?" That was the moment I completely lost faith and believed there was no God and if he did exist, then he was a cruel child who loved to kick his toys.

When I came back into the apartment, Lilith was up and sitting at my desk, looking at my computer. She asked me to keep an open mind about the request she was going to make. I listened to her ludicrous request, but out of love and desperation, I agreed to it.

Her obsession with mythology and Colonial history also included in-depth knowledge of the occult in America. Lilith wanted to try a séance in Fenway where her research said there is a place where deals can be made with the supernatural. I didn't believe in that stuff and under normal circumstances I would have thought she was delusional, but I desperately wanted for her to be happy before she died. I agreed, and we planned a romantic getaway to Fenway that weekend.

We spent the beautiful fall day exploring the town and taking the history tours she likes. Coincidentally, it was All Hallows Eve, and the town was in full Halloween spirit with its decorations, kids wearing superhero costumes and the Crossroads Pub packed with costumed adults who were drunk and enjoying the debauchery. I saw a smile come across Lilith's face as she basked in the jovial and macabre ether of the night. I also smiled, almost forgetting about her cancer until she bent over and began coughing violently into her handkerchief. She looked up at me and I saw the blood smear her lips and the handkerchief. The grim reality made itself known again.

With the sun setting, we made our way out past the party and through the cemetery where we saw a couple in Kanye West and a Kim Kardashian costumes having sex on a grave. We hiked into the woods, deep enough where the music and the lights from the Pub were just a glimpse away but far enough where nobody would see us. Lilith pulled out of her backpack a lantern, a few candles, a raggedy notebook, and a dagger. Dim yellow light fluttered out of the lantern as she placed the candles in a circle, lighting them as she softly chanted. She opened her notebook and began talking in a language I have never heard.

When I agreed to do this, I was only doing it to humor her, but now a cold chill went down my spine and my stomach cringed with fright. The wind began to blow harder, and the light and music from the Pub faded away as if we were alone on an island in the dark. I asked her to stop, but she kept speaking in a frightening language. I grabbed her arm and spun her around and found her eyes were black voids and her skin colder than a corpse. Before I could react to the ghastly sight, I felt something sinister and omnipresent behind me. I turned around and that's when I saw the great-grotesque Beast. At that moment I felt as if I was in a lucid nightmare in which I was floating and had no control of my body.

Lucifer spoke in a deep and earthshaking tone and asked me, "Would you sell your soul for her to live a life everlasting?"

I looked over and saw her body floating too with blood coming out of her mouth. Without a doubt, I said, "I do."

Lucifer roared, "So be it, Llewyn Glass. You will have one year from today to enjoy your life before I come to collect my due. So, you may never forget our agreement, may your shadow always cast in front of you so it can be a constant reminder of the debt you must pay."

The Beast looked over to Lilith and said, "Well done. You have got what you wanted after all."

With that, I fell hard to the ground and was knocked unconscious.

The warmth from the early morning sun awoke me and I found Lilith asleep a few feet away from me. Hoping it was just a horrible nightmare, I crawled over to her and held her in my arms. She slowly opened her eyes and smiled, but it wasn't a smile of warmth, but a wicked one. Lilith pushed me away from her and jumped up onto her feet. She spread her arms into the warm rays of the dawn and yelled, "I did it!" She danced as I slowly picked myself up and re-oriented myself.

"What did you do?" I asked grimly.

She strutted toward me and said, "You stupid boy. I can't believe you sold your soul to the Devil. But I have to thank you for your sacrifice because now I am going to live forever."

The sudden emotions of confusion and heartbreak overwhelmed me, and I fell to my knees. Lilith pulled my chin up. "You look so pathetic and confused, let me clear this up for you. I...used...you." She let go of my chin, and I collapsed on the grassy ground.

"Still confused? What is the one thing we all want? Immortality. I tried to make this deal with the Morning Star last year, and he told me that I did not have anything he wanted because I was destined to spend eternity in hell. I don't need to go over the particulars why but let's say I deserved to go. But thanks to you, sweetie, I am not going anywhere. He told me that if I can get a good man who was forsaken for doing right and get him to give him his soul freely, then I can be immortal."

"Fortunately, the next day you came up in the news for ratting on that corrupt filth of an organization, and I knew I had found my soul. I knew it wouldn't be hard to have you fall for me, a virgin who had never touched a woman because of his petty oath to God. But I needed you to fall deeply love with me so I could get you desperate enough to do anything for me... then again, you're a man, so that was easy. All I had to do was fuck you good and listen to you bitch and moan about your stupid church and justice. But, to get you to follow through willingly, I needed a good con."

Lilith walked over to her backpack and retrieved the dagger and a small container. She threw the container at me, it landed in front of my face. It was a packet of fake blood capsules for Halloween. She never had cancer. My disorientation turned into rage as I picked myself up and charged at her but I stopped when she pointed the dagger at me.

"No, no, no, sweetie. You would never hit a woman, especially one you can't hurt." She suddenly took the dagger and plunged it into her stomach. Lilith looked up and smiled as she pulled out the bloody dagger from her stomach and the hole closed and healed itself. I was in shock and couldn't move. I couldn't tell what sickened me the most: the idea of going to hell or the heartbreak and betrayal.

"You're truly are a pathetic man. Look at you, who would love you? You don't even love yourself enough to see that the one thing you should never give away is your soul."

After her cruel words, I stormed toward her, wrapped my hands around her neck and lifted her off of the ground as I tried to end her immortality with whatever strength I had left.

"You bitch! You conned me!" I screamed with gobs of spit and tears spurting up on her passive face, which only made me squeeze harder. "I lost my soul! You took that away from me! You fucking betrayed me! Did you even love me?"

With the last question, I felt her windpipe crush between my hands, and I dropped her limp body. Lilith lay lifeless as the intense agony of having killed her overwhelmed me. I knelt down beside her, lifted her into my arms and began to cry.

"Why? Why did you do this?" I cried.

Lilith's head suddenly jolted, she gasped for air, and said, "Because I can."

Defeated, I knelt there, speechless, and forever lost. Lilith picked herself up, brushed the leaves off of her clothing and stood there smiling. "Not only did I got you to sell your soul, but I broke you also. The man who will do what is right at all cost just "killed" his ex-lover. You truly are pathetic. But then again, you were a good fuck for a 30-year-old virgin."

I knelt there in shock as she took those final steps out of my life and through the woods. I couldn't, I wouldn't believe what happened to me. I was numb as I stood there in the middle of the woods for God knows how long, kneeling as the pain meticulously worked its way into my heart and I finally imploded in emotion. The betrayal, the heartbreak, and ultimately the realization of what was going to happen on Halloween next year hit me like a sledgehammer to my stomach as I collapsed on the ground and began uncontrollably crying.

The rising sun's rays begin to trickle through the forest and warmed my cold face. I adjusted my eyes and noticed something odd. My shadow was being cast on the ground in front of me instead of behind me, and no matter which way I turned, my shadow was constantly in front of me. A reminder of my curse.

The heavy rain on the way back to Boston mirrored the overwhelming sadness and despair I felt inside. I was starving but I didn't have the strength to even chew a sandwich I bought from the gas station. All I wanted to do was to go home and sleep.

When I finally made it back, I found the apartment devoid of her things except for a packet of fake blood capsules propped in the middle of the floor with my shadow eclipsing them. I collapsed on the floor and cried. The overwhelming thoughts of the futility of my cursed existence coupled with betrayal and heartbreak plagued my head for days as I lay on that floor, wallowing in pity and regret. I did not leave my home for weeks, ordering out for food, staring at my shadow and living in filth as I lost all hope. I turned to the bottle for comfort and to numb the pain. The bottle gave me the courage to finally leave my home, but it only led me to bars where I kept drinking and drinking. But the reoccurring feelings of dread and heartbreak kept haunting me, so I bought pain pills to numb them.

Though heartbroken and lonely, I dreadfully wanted the touch of another woman, but my feeble attempts stemming from my misery only turned off any woman I talked to, and each rejection made me weaker and more bitter inside.

"I'm going to hell anyway," I thought to myself as I ordered prostitutes to my apartment one after another. They only granted me a moment of satisfaction and pleasure but it never lasted but I kept fucking to stop the pain. I wanted something more than just meaningless sex, but I no longer thought myself worthy of another person's love, not even my own.

Four months into my plunge of dissolution and despair, I had left a brothel drunk and was about to enter a bar when I saw a reflection of myself in a puddle on the sidewalk. I took a long good look at myself and felt despair over who I had become. What happened to me? I was a fighter. I was brave. I took on challenges that were bigger than me and didn't care about failure, just did them to fight and to become something more than what I was. Now a broken man's drunk face stared back with the smell of Jack Daniels and the musk of a whore coming off of me.

My eyes stopped focusing on my reflection and onto my shadow in front of me, the constant reminder of my doom, and I heard the deep voice of Johnny Cash and the holy strums of his guitar from the bar playing, "The Man that Comes Around."

I had listened to this song countless times, but at that moment in my life, it spoke to my soul. His powerful chords and lyrics no longer made me feel pity or hopelessness but fueled a flame made dim from the pain. It rekindled my old soul as I looked down upon my poor reflection and the shadow that haunted me and I became determined, brave again. I was more than the man who was staring back at me, and I wasn't going to go down like this. I wasn't going to hell without giving a fight. I'm going to get my soul back. I'm going to beat the Devil.

I went back home to start finding a way out of this. I didn't know where to start, but I opened up my laptop and before I could begin researching, I received an email from the Vatican titled, "Come to Rome."

Come to Rome immediately, Mr. Glass. I know what happened and I need to help you. Attached is your flight information. I don't need to remind you about your deadline.

Sincerely,

Sister Abigail LeFay

Director of Antiquities, Anthropology, and History

Vatican City, Italy.

How did she know about what happened and why wait now to help me? Is this a trick? Can she really help me? I took a moment to breathe and recollect myself, but that moment quickly passed as I found myself opening my safe and retrieving my passport.

Sister Abigail LeFay of the Vatican

Rome, Italy. February 14, 2015

I was nursing a hangover with an awful helping of jet lag when I finally made it to Rome Central Station, the bright sun making my headache even worse. I wished I was still taking the pain meds, but I needed to be clear-headed when I visited Sister Abigail. I hailed a taxi and said one word, "Vatican."

The taxi driver drove fast and cut cars off through the traffic as we made our way across the city, over a bridge, and past the massive castle of Castel Sant' Angelo, where I looked up to see the statue of St. Michael, his wings spread and his sword drawn over the castle. Maybe he was available to help me out.

The taxi dropped me off among the swarms of tourists in front of St. Peter's Square. Lines were stretching across the front of the massive city-state, but I walk out of the square and followed the high walls and columns surrounding the Vatican.

I made a turn around a secluded corner and found the visitor entrance with the Swiss Guards standing in front with their assault rifles. I slowly walked over to the guard booth and presented my passport as he checked for my name on the visitor's list.

The two guards with the rifles kept glancing over at me, likely recognizing me as the "Forsaken Priest." The guard in the booth cleared me, and I walked past them and into a large garden behind St. Peter's Basilica. A warm nostalgia embraced me as I remembered the first time coming here as a young man pursuing a higher calling, but the dismissive, angry stares from the priest and the

Swiss Guard made me regret coming. They must have felt good about themselves as I looked like I'd fallen from grace.

I walked into the bright yellow archaic building and made my way to the front desk where I was checked again, given a visitor pass, and then escorted to the elevator where we descended three stories below the Vatican. We walked out of the elevator and into a musty, dirt-floored, and wooden beamed corridor that reminded me of an old wine cellar.

The guard led me to a newly installed oak door, gently rapped his knuckles on the door, and announced in Italian that I was here. The door swung open, and I saw the warm smile of a gray-haired woman who I could safely assume to be Sister Abigail. She gave the guard a gentle kiss on each cheek and thanked him for escorting me, then wrapped her arms around me, she squeezed me tight before kissing me on each cheek. Her smile was infectious and for the first time in a long time, my cheeks hurt from grinning back to her.

"Come in," she said cheerfully in her Tennessee accent. She led me into her office which also functioned as an archive with rows of leather-bound books, relics, and art filling the high vaulted walls. We walked over to her desk, but she stopped me before I could sit down and lifted up a flashlight.

"May I?" she asked as she already knew about my shadow.

I nodded, and she walked around me several times as she shined the flashlight on me, my shadow always casting in front no matter where she shined the light.

"Fascinating," she said curiously to herself.

I snapped at her, "Not to be rude, but nothing is fucking fascinating about this."

She looked up in shock from my language, but before I could apologize for my rudeness, she waved her hand and said, "I understand. Your time is limited, and you need help, which I convinced the Vatican to do so without any remorse to you."

"Thank you. But, how do you know about my curse? Was the Vatican keeping tabs on me? Spying on me?"

"The Vatican, no. Myself, yes. And it wasn't you I was spying on. It was Lilith."

"Lilith?" I said as a whirlwind of confusion and dread consumed me. "Why would you spy on her?"

Sister Abigail walked behind her large, antique desk and sat in the well-worn leather office chair for a moment in silence, contemplating her next words. "I have been spying on Lilith for two reasons: My position in the Vatican requires me to monitor and classify certain unique individuals, creatures, and sites. The second is..." she paused as she took a sigh of despair "she is my daughter."

"Daughter? How can that be? You're a Nun, you took the same vows of chastity we all had to take. Are you a hypocrite like the others in this godforsaken organization?"

"No, I have been faithful to God and the Church, but I wasn't always a Nun. What I am about to tell you is the truth, and it is a secret that only God knows. It is painful for me to tell you this, but I want and need to help you, so you deserve the whole truth."

I sat back in the chair across from her, took out a flask and a cigarette and began consuming the fire from each. I gestured if she wanted a sip and she took the offer, taking a shot of whiskey without making a face.

"I was not always Sister Abigail LeFay, I was once Doctor Abigail LeFay, Ph. D. I was a Tennessee country girl who made her way into Boston University on hard work, waiting tables and a ton of scholarships. At 28 I was on top of the world. I had just earned my Doctorate in Anthropology after doing my dissertation on Native American tribes and their use of hallucinogens in religious ceremonies. It was a wonderful time for me, and I felt on top of the world. I was young, pretty, and loved to have fun. I would drink men twice my size underneath the table and then go into the office the next day to continue my research. I loved my life until the unfortunate morning 29 years ago." Sister Abigail stared off in the distance and took a long swig from the flask.

"I slept in my office on campus after a night of researching and grading students' papers, and I awakened to the bright rays of the early dawn coming through my office window. I didn't have any classes to teach until the late afternoon, so I decided to go home and get some rest. It was still early, and there was no one on campus as I walked to the parking lot. When I made it to my car, I felt the hairs on the back of my neck stand up and heard something behind me. I turned around and standing at the rear of my car was a large man with a sinister look. I fiddled with my keys to get my mini pepper spray, but it was too late. Before I was able to think about running, he leaped from the back of my car and pinned me against it. I screamed and started scratching his face, but he punched me in the jaw, and it stunned me enough to fall against the car. He opened my rear door and threw me in the back seat and..."

She paused and I felt the pain coming from her eyes as she briefly looked at me before turning her chair away from me. "I think I don't need to tell you what happened next."

"No, you don't have to relive it again," I said, hoping to comfort her.

Sister Abigail didn't speak for a few moments and then she took another swig from the flask and continued. "They never caught him. This was a time when DNA testing wasn't established, and the campus had no security cameras. He was gone, but he left something within me, his unborn child. I didn't realize I was pregnant until a month in because I was devastated and suffering from so much fear and shame from the rape that I was in denial. I went mad with grief and disgust when I found out I was pregnant with his baby. His seed was growing in me. He had not only robbed me of a normal life but now he left me with a reminder of how evil he was."

"At the time, I wasn't religious. I hadn't been to church since I was a little girl and I felt like I didn't need it. I never felt guilty about anything I'd done up to that point in my life until I decided to have an abortion."

"You tried to abort Lilith?" I asked as sensitively as possible, although the thought looming in the back of my head wished she had.

Sister Abigail finished off the flask before going quiet for a moment again and sternly said, "Yes. When I went to the doctor and was about to go through with the abortion, I thought for a moment that this life inside of me didn't ask for it to be forced inside me.
It didn't deserve to die, it wasn't the baby's fault, and it deserved a chance on this planet. I stopped the kind doctor, who understood and helped me get in touch with an adoption agency. I chose for her to live but I couldn't live with her as a constant reminder of the rape. The Thornes, a kind and well-to-do family in Cambridge were chosen as her new family. They never knew the circumstances of how she was conceived, but they could tell from my face when I met them that I was

traumatized. The day I gave birth to her was

to have her out of my life and hopeful tha

awful giving birth, it was so painful, a

me cursing him for doing this to me

I cursed God, and I cursed the baby; .

time, a powerful joy swept through me. I looke

her. The doctor placed her small, shivering body in my a.

because I knew that was the only moment I will have with her wh.

tainted by the memory of my rapist. I kissed her on the head and had Miste.

Mrs. Thorne come and take her from me. They named her Lilith Morgania, a

Gaelic name.

"Knowing what I been through and not wanting the physical touch of a

man ever again, I left my academic post and joined a convent. At first, I used the

convent as an escape from the pain of my rape and the deep sadness and guilt over

giving away my daughter, but then I felt as if I found my calling. After my

postulancy, I chose to become a Nun and devote my life to something beyond

myself. Even though I don't agree with the Catholic Church at times, I have found

solace in serving others. Word spread about my academic pedigree, and I was

invited to join the Vatican's Department of Antiquities, Anthropology, and

History. Within ten years I was the first Nun in history to be placed in charge of

the department, and it gave me great influence and resources at my disposal.

"During all this time of advancing my life, I thought about Lilith every

day and wondered what she was doing. It wasn't until she was sixteen that I finally

decided to see her. I made some calls; you would know out of all people how deep

the influence the Catholic Church's connections are. I was able to find the Thornes

oston. I left the Vatican and flown back to the states, not
idea of what to say or do when I saw her again. I drove my
eir neighborhood and parked down the street for a few hours. I was
d thoughts about seeing her and almost decided to drive back to the

"Then, I saw her walk out the door, and I saw how beautiful she had
come. I couldn't control my crying; she looked like me when I was her age. The
Thornes had helped her grow into a wonderful young woman, and she looked
remarkable. Lilith was walking toward me, and I begin to panic, but I forgot I was
in civilian clothes and a rental car. She walked past me without giving me a
glance, and my heart trembled as she turned the corner and left my sight again. I
didn't move for an hour until I had an idea of how I would approach her. The next
day I wore my Nun garb and waited in the same corner. I waited there for an hour
until I saw Lilith walking toward me. I hid my nervousness as she came to the
corner and I put on an act as a lost Nun sightseeing in Boston. To my delight, she
helped me out, and we talked for a few minutes and even walked together for a
while. She invited me to accompany her to a coffee shop where she often went to
study. She was graduating early from high school and was getting a scholarship to
Harvard. I couldn't be happier for her.

It seemed like Lilith was on the right track and she hadn't become a
maladjusted woman like I feared she would. We talked for hours until I worked
up the courage to tell her the truth. She knew she was adopted but the Thornes lost
track of me, but she always wondered who I was.

"She seemed solemn as I told her that I was her mother but then she asked
why I abandoned her and that's when I couldn't do it. I couldn't tell her the truth.

I lied and told her that I had gotten drunk at a party and had sex with a man I never saw again. I put her up for adoption because I was young and afraid. Her solemn face turned to rage and quietly, without bringing attention to us in the coffee shop, cursed me and called me a selfish cunt. The young woman who I had begun to admire was showing me a dark and malevolent side, and it was frightening to me. I tried to calm her, but she took out her phone and showed me pictures which nearly caused me to faint.

"Is this where my sick shit comes from?" She showed me pictures of mutilated animals and screenshots of dead bodies. I couldn't understand what was happening, Lilith was a monster in disguise, and she blamed me for her illness.

I was distraught and disgusted with her tales of torturing the neighborhood pets since she was a kid, manipulating her parents, classmates, and teachers, and even suffocating her baby sister when she first came home because she was jealous of the attention the newborn was receiving. I asked her why she did all of this and she simply said, "Because, I can."

"My worst fears had come true. My daughter was a creature of evil like the man who raped me. I threatened to go to the police, but she simply laughed and said I couldn't because I wouldn't be able to substantiate anything she told me. She saw me nervously fidget with my rosary beads and whisper a silent prayer.

"She reached with her hand and stopped me from praying. "No, no. There isn't any help from the indifferent creator," she said with an uneasy truth hitting me in the gut. She got up and walked away as I sat there crying.

'I left for Rome the next day, but on the flight back I read an email from my connection in Boston that her house caught fire and her parents died that very night. I had given birth to a monster."

Sister Abigail had tears rolling down her face, but her stoic expression remained the same.

"Why didn't you tell her that you were raped?" I asked.

"How can you tell someone that they weren't meant to be on this planet? That they were conceived in a horrible and gruesome act. That they were such a burden that I came close to aborting them but then last minute decided to let them live. How would you feel if you heard that?" she said crying.

We both sat quietly in a sobering silence.

"How did you know about what happened to me and why is the Catholic Church interested in helping the man that exposed them?"

"That's my job. What the world knows, and you use to believe, is that the supernatural and the divine are metaphorical. Lore and myths are stories misinterpreted by the deluded and the uneducated and later disavowed by logic and science. But, as you know now, the supernatural exists in the peripheral of reality, and the Catholic Church along with other major religions, scientists, and government agencies have proof of this. The Vatican's Department of Antiquities, Anthropology, and History is in charge of investigating these phenomena and classifying them from the public. Before you ask why keep it a secret, it's because the others and I have agreed that the world isn't ready to know the truth."

"Why not?" I said perplexed and awed. "If there is proof of God and the Devil, why hide it from the world?"

"Because we don't understand what the truth is. All over the world, we find that major parts of myths and legends did and still exist in the world. There are deities living among us, monsters that still haunt us, and mysteries we cannot comprehend. If we tell the world that these things exist then the religious culture wars we had over the past millennia would look like a schoolyard fight compared to what travesties the governments and religions of the world will commit upon each other to prove whose god is more powerful. Just imagine the Crusades but with nukes and biological weapons. We agreed to keep these a secret and pool our resources together to understand what we see until..."

"Until the Church can spin it the way it wants, to hold their power. To let the world know that you know what's best for it?" I said cynically.

"Not when I'm in charge. I will let the world know when my counterparts and I have agreed what the facts are. Then we will release the facts and let the world choose what to believe. But the other scientist, monks, Rabbis, etc. and I cannot do so in good conscience."

For a moment I started to believe and even trust her but then she still hasn't answered my question. "How did you know about my deal?"

"Isn't obvious? Once promoted to Director, I classified Lilith as a person of interest due to her sociopathic behavior and kept tabs on her. She gained an interest in the occult, but I never thought she would render a manifestation or become entwined with the supernatural. It wasn't until we were made aware of ritualistic murders around Boston that I became more involved with Lilith again, especially with one on a hallow site in the town of Fenway. On a gut feeling, I sent an operative to spy on her and he reported back to me that he witnessed Lilith, you, and a creature so horrifying that the mere sight of it caused a shock so intense that he did not awake from his coma until a few days ago. I immediately contacted you as soon as he told us what happened, hence why you are sitting across from me in a country that has forsaken you."

"But why help me? You know there is no saving me from what I did, and this hypocritical institution would love to see me literally go to hell."

"Because I see the good in you. You're a good man who became lost after tragedies of a broken heart. You believed in justice and what is right, which underlies all beliefs; a universal truth which you never swayed from even the face of adversity. Then you loved another enough to sacrifice your soul to save her life, to save my daughter. You are damned, unforgivable in the eyes of God, but I am going to use whatever influence I have to help you get your soul back and find your way out of the gates of hell."

For the first time in a long time, I felt hope. "What happens now?"

Sister Abigail opened the drawer to her desk and pulled out a bottle of scotch and two glasses. She filled them both to the rim and handed me one. We both drank the savory scotch, but she finished hers in one gulp.

"Mister Glass, I am sending you down the road of mystery and wonder, of gods and monsters. You will witness and experience things which go beyond science and belief. You are walking in between worlds, between what we know and what we could never have fathomed. Be careful on this path you blaze because you might find a fate worse than hell."

The Old Gypsy

Rome, Italy. February 14th, 2015.

I walked from the Vatican through the narrow and busy streets of Rome to the Coliseum. I took my time because I was instructed by Sister Abigail to wait until midnight to meet with her source. Even though it was late, the tourists were still out eating and drinking, and street hustlers were still trying to sell their Selfie-sticks, but the sites were even more beautiful at night. Especially when the night lights hit Trevi Fountain; they reflected a brilliant white and blue hue that made the statues seem that the gods blessed them.

I stood outside the closed Coliseum and waited for a man named Jal. I didn't mind the wait because the Coliseum was beautiful underneath the full moon. Even though it was in ruins, I could not help but admire the feat the ancient Romans had built. It was massive and mesmerizing. It was hard for me to fathom how they created this elaborate structure without today's technology. Even though it is slowly becoming decrepit from age and the vibrations from the underground trains, it's astonishing that it still stands.

A cold hand touched my shoulder, and I swung around out of fright. A smiling brown face in a security guard's uniform greeted me. "Are you Llewyn?" he said in a heavy Italian accent.

"Si."

"Ciao, I am Jal. Sister Abigail called me and told me about your...issue. Follow me and let's see if we can find you some answers."

"We?"

"Si, my grandmother, is inside. She is the one with the gift."

"What gift?"

"You'll see," he said as he led me to the gate of the Coliseum. He checked first to see if the gate was locked and then pulled out a set of keys from his pocket and unlocked it.

Jal led me inside and locked the gate behind me. I looked up at massive columns and high stone ceilings which still rival modern-day stadiums. We walked past the visitor entrances into the arena of the Coliseum and took a back entrance into the underground levels. Jal lit a lantern that was sitting at the top of a stone staircase and led me down the dark corridors.

Through the dim flickering light, I could see the old rooms where they kept the gladiators, weapons, and animals, but now only held extra chairs and tables for special events. I found it strange that after all these years I could still smell the faint coppery odor of blood in the air. We went deeper into the Coliseum where we entered the level beneath the arena. Above our heads was a partial replica of the arena floor where they would have the violent battles and spectacles. The other half of the arena was open to the night sky where the full moon's light lit our path to a small person in the center of the arena.

"Mi grandmother," Jal said as we walked toward her.

Jal gave her a hug and then a kiss on each cheek. She was a small petite woman wearing a brown and red dress with a yellow headcover. She had an old redwood cane with demons and skeletons carved into the lower half and angels and doves in the top half. She had a hunch back, her hands were thin, and her knuckles enlarged. Her face had a dark complexion with deep wrinkles, but she had brilliant blue eyes that were vibrant for someone her age. Jal spoke to her in a language I have never heard before.

"We are Romani...uh, Gypsies is what you might hear my people called. Before you ask, I got a job here because I wanted my child to live in a proper home. This here is my grandmother, Nadya."

"Ciao," I said as I kissed her on each cheek.

"She only speaks Romani, so I'll be doing the translating."

She spoke to him for a few moments and pointed to the lantern in his hand and then to me.

"She wants to see if it is true what Sister Abigail said about your curse." As he lifted the lantern in front of me, the light produced a shadow directly ahead of me, even as he walked around me with the lantern.

Nadya did not seem troubled or surprised by this. She gave an expression as if she had seen much stranger things in her life. She spoke to Jal in Romani again as she reached into her small satchel and handed him a knife, at which I instinctively stepped back. She then turned around and looked at the ground. I had not seen it when we walked up but there was large pentagram drawn in chalk below our feet with Latin letters written around it.

"She wants a piece of your hair," as he handed me the knife.

Relieved, I lifted the knife behind my head and cut a small patch off from the back of my neck and gave him the strands. He took the hair and placed it in a bowl lying on the ground.

"What are we doing here and what is with the pentagram?" I asked.

Jal translated to Nadya and spoke something back to him. "She says we can't break your curse, much too powerful and dark magic. But, we are going to summon someone to help you."

"O.K..." I said perplexed.

Nadya began speaking again as she took a piece of chalk and attached it to the bottom of her cane and continued writing in Latin on the ground.

"First, we must tell you his story."

"Whose?"

"The spirit we are summoning. His name is Hakīm and he lived around 80 A.D."

"Why do we need Hakīm's story?" I asked frustrated.

Jal translated my question as Nadya took the bowl with my hair in it and mixed it with some herbs she had in her pocket.

"She says his story will help you understand the advice Hakīm's spirit will give you when he arrives. Now she says, uh...how do you say it in American? Silenzio the fuck up and listen."

Nadya gave me a piercing look with those vibrant eyes of hers; I relented and sat down on the dirt and listened to the story.

Hakīm was a Moor who lived here in Rome during the reign of Caesar Domitain. He traveled the known world and learned medicine from different cultures and brought his knowledge to Rome as a doctor. Hakīm treated all people from different classes and took any form of payment they could offer him, and he never turned down anyone in need. His medical skills and kindness were renowned throughout Rome, for which Caesar requested him to come to his court. Hakīm went to Caesar and listened to his proposition: come work for him as his physician, and he'll make him powerful and wealthy. Hakīm was not a man who sought riches nor power but was a simple man who enjoyed helping others. He asked if he would still be able to treat the ill and wounded of Rome, at which Caesar said no. Caesar wanted him available at any time if he or those closest to him became ill. Hakīm wished to continue his current life respectfully declined. Caesar was enraged, for he wanted the best medical care easily accessible to him since he traveled extensively across the empire and had suspicions of an imminent assassination. Hakīm paid his respects to Caesar and was about to leave when Caesar ordered the guards to stop him. Caesar decided if he could not have the Moor doctor then no one would and sentenced him to public execution. Hakīm was a pacifist and abhorred violence, but he was wise and intelligent and made a bold suggestion. Instead of execution let him win back his freedom in the Coliseum by fighting the gladiators.

Caesar's interest peaked as Hakīm made an even bolder proposition, if he won three battles in the arena without killing he wished to be set free and allowed to return to his profession in Rome. Caesar thought about it for a moment; such a bold proposition, to win in the Coliseum without shedding blood. He eyed Hakīm's slender frame and knew that he was not built for any battle. Caesar was intrigued by the notion, accepted the deal and sent Hakīm to the Coliseum for the games.

Hakīm took part in his first challenge on the following day. He was brought into the middle of the hot and sweltering arena wearing ill-fitting armor while holding a heavy shield and a dull sword. From his royal stand, Caesar arrogantly boasted to the crowd about Hakim's dilemma. The crowd cheered and laughed. How could a man win against the gladiators without killing? Especially someone who looks like Hakīm.

The trumpets blasted to signal the arrival of Hakīm's opponent, the Leviathan. The Leviathan was a vicious looking massive man who was three times the size of Hakīm, fitted with durable armor and given the sharpest sword. The Leviathan was known for his brutal fighting and drinking the blood of his opponents from his helmet.

Both the Leviathan and Hakīm met in the middle of the arena and the crowd fell silent. Before the horn blast was given to fight, Hakīm plunged his sword into the ground and dropped his shield and began stripping off all his armor. Caesar and the crowd became collectively confused by the sight while the Leviathan started to chuckle underneath his heavy armor. Hakīm stripped down to his tunic and retrieved only his shield from the ground and stood ready for the battle. Caesar, still confused by Hakīm's act, ordered the fight to begin and watched eagerly from his stand.

The Leviathan raised his heavy sword and prepared to strike, but Hakīm kept moving away from his reach forcing the Leviathan to keep advancing.

The Leviathan would swing his sword, but Hakīm would keep moving backward causing him to miss. The Leviathan, no longer amused, began running after him and slashing his sword violently at Hakīm. But Hakīm just ran and led the Leviathan on a chase around the grand arena. Hakīm would slow down and taunt the Leviathan by letting him take a swing and hitting Hakīm's shield, then he would begin the chase again after. The crowd kept laughing at the comical sight as the massive gladiator chased the small man but Caesar knew better, for he was a general and realized the brilliant tactic Hakīm was performing against his opponent.

This chase went on for a few more minutes and the Leviathan grew visibly exhausted. The hot sun heated his bronze armor, his feet dragged from the heavy armor and his sword swings were few and low while Hakīm would slow down just enough to give him a false opportunity to strike. The Leviathan, unaware of Hakīm's tactic, would still take the chance, miss, and give chase again. The Leviathan, out of pride or stupidity, would not relent on chasing Hakīm until his legs gave out from underneath him and he fell to his knees, violently vomiting from heat exhaustion.

The Leviathan panicked and could not breathe underneath his armor as he erratically threw off his helmet. Hakīm saw the opportunity he was waiting for and ran around the Leviathan until he was behind him, raised his shield and bashed it against the back of the Leviathan's head. The Leviathan lay on the ground unconscious as Hakīm attended to his opponent and treated him in front of the awed crowd. Caesar had unknowingly been standing up the whole time from sheer astonishment, and he reluctantly declared Hakīm the winner of his first battle.

The following day Hakīm faced his next challenge as he was brought into the middle of the arena and quickly abandoned by the guards who ran behind the closed gates. Hakīm was puzzled by the sudden departure as he stood in the center wearing only his tunic. The crowd became silent as they wondered what was taking place until they heard the loud barking and howling coming from one of the corridors. Hakīm spun around and saw a pack of wolves was now behind the corridor's gates.

Large gray wolves with bloodied fangs were savagely snapping at the iron gate, hoping to taste Hakīm's flesh. His heart raced as the gates slowly began to rise and the wolves were eagerly digging their paws underneath the gate and snarling at Hakīm.

Hakīm looked around the arena and saw no weapon or a place to hide. This is the first time the crowd and Caesar saw Hakīm fear for his life. The gates barely rose when the first three of the pack crawled underneath and charged towards Hakīm. He had a moment of dread as the wolves came closer to him until an idea came to him; he merely brought his hands to his side and stood still.

The wolves stopped their charge a mere few feet away from him and began to snarl and bark at him, but he did not move. The other five wolves of the pack came running and started circling him. They too snarled and barked at Hakīm, but he did not move. The pack leader came close and snapped at his hands, but Hakīm did not flinch. All he did was stand still and focus on his breathing. The sight silenced the crowd for they feared a sudden noise might cause the wolves to attack. Caesar became dumbfounded by the act as he could not comprehend why the wolves were not ripping him apart.

Hakīm stood in the center of the arena surrounded by the pack of vicious wolves for an hour, but he did not move. The wolves grew bored of him; some laid down around him while others walked around the arena. Caesar became angered by Hakīm's cleverness and ordered the guards to leave him and the wolves there for the night, hoping he would grow tired and let the wolves attack. With that Caesar and the crowd retreated for the night.

The next morning Caesar eagerly rode to the Coliseum to see the carnage from the night before. A cheering and awed crowd greeted him. Caesar looked down into the arena and saw Hakīm sitting on the ground petting the now docile wolves that were sleeping around him.

Caesar was so angered and baffled from what he was witnessing from the defiant Moor and so he devised a spectacular game not only to entertain the crowd but to finally kill Hakīm. During Caesar Domitain's reign, the Coliseum had the means to flood the arena floor with water from canals so the arena could host lavish naval battles. Hakīm's final challenge would be one man versus a Roman ship of war.

Hakīm had two days to prepare as the arena was flooded with water for the battle. Caesar being spiteful, only gave Hakīm a small rowboat to go against a scaled-down version of a trireme with a crew of 30 war-worn sailors, a row of rowers on each side and large white sails to show off the majesty of the Roman Navy. Caesar wanted to see a fight, so he gave Hakīm access to any weapon to use in what was sure to be a slaughter. Hakīm did not choose any weapon but only stared at the trireme, studying it, scheming a plan to beat a warship. It wasn't until the morning of the battle that Hakīm requested his weapons of choice: a bow and a few arrows, three jars of oil; a couple of chunks of fat from a cow, and a piece of flint.

The crowd fell silent as the massive trireme sailed into the arena, the rowers rowing in sync with the heart-pounding melody of the war drums, its large white sails with Caesar Domitain's seal fluttering with the wind as it made its grand entrance. The crowd was in awe but then broke out in laughter as Hakīm rowed his small dingy into the arena; one man and his odd assortment of weapons against Rome's most excellent sailors.

Caesar rose from his stand, and the crowd fell silent as he gave a wave of his hand to signal the beginning of the battle. The trireme's oars ripped through the water as the trireme maneuvered to attack Hakīm who was floating at the other end of the arena.

The sailors were jovial and relaxed as they were in no rush to destroy the helpless man in his small dingy and Hakīm was strangely calm as he slowly tied chunks of fat to the heads of the arrows. As the trireme made its way into the middle of the arena, Hakīm took a piece of flint and lit the fat on the arrows, which blazed with fire, and began shooting them at the boat. The crowd and Caesar gasped in silence as the flaming arrows hit the sails and fire quickly engulfed them. The sailors stopped rowing as panic fell upon them while flaming pieces of canvas fell on the deck and heavy smoke filled their lungs. As they were distracted by the fire, Hakīm rowed his dingy next to the trireme, and one by one hurled the jars of oil onto the deck. The oil now saturated the deck unbeknownst to the sailors who were futility trying to extinguish the flames.

One sailor looked down at the oil and realized in terror what Hakīm had done and ordered the men to abandoned ship. Just as the sailors were jumping off the ship, a flaming patch of canvas fell onto the oily deck and ignited the entire ship into a bright orange blaze. Hakīm, showing no emotion, slowly rowed away as the sailors swam to the edges of the arena and the ship slowly began to sink and the Coliseum filled with smoke.

The crowd coughed and wheezed, but they chanted Hakīm's name while Caesar's face grew red from both the excessive coughing and his fury over Hakīm foiling him once again. Caesar did not want the Moor to escape his grasp, so he announced to the crowd that he added one last challenge for him: if he can survive a hanging, then Hakīm would be set free. The crowd reluctantly applauded as they felt that Caesar was cruel over losing to the masterful tactician, but Hakīm did not give Caesar the satisfaction of showing any emotion to his public betrayal.

The night before the public hanging, Hakīm went to the Coliseum's blacksmith and asked him for a thin and porous pipe.

The blacksmith, perplexed by the odd request, reshaped a pipe to Hakīm's satisfaction. Hakīm took the pipe and did something that made the blacksmith gasped in shock.

The morning of the hanging Hakīm was brought into the arena below Caesar's box and stripped naked to make sure he was not hiding any clever tricks for an escape. The crowd was silent and did not applaud when Caesar arose, for they felt Hakīm had earned his freedom and Caesar was now acting cruelly. A wooden scaffold was ceremoniously wheeled out and brought to where Hakīm stood. The hangman wrapped the noose around Hakīm's neck and tightened it, but he did not flinch or show any expression of terror or remorse. Caesar asked if he had any final words, but Hakīm was silently defiant. The order was given and the rope slowly hoisted Hakīm off the ground as the crowd began to cry and looked away from the man that was the bloodless warrior. He did not kick or flop or even cry as his eyes slowly closed for the final time. The crowd fell silent as time passed but there was no more movement from his body.

Caesar felt tremendous guilt come over him for he had killed a wonderful man who was only guilty of having a brilliant mind and unwavering character. Caesar ordered the hangman to cut down the body and give Hakīm a proper burial. The hangman cut the rope, and the body fell hard onto the ground. Disgusted with himself, Caesar began to leave his box until the crowd gave out a loud cheer of excitement.

Caesar looked down in shock as he saw Hakīm slowly standing up. After seeing the impossible, Caesar now feared Hakīm because no mortal man could have won the challenges placed in front of him; and now he had survived death. Hakīm slowly walked to the open gate out of the arena as the hangman and soldiers looked onto Caesar for his next order, but he was still in shock. Fearing he might anger the gods; Caesar gave the order for Hakīm to be set free and the crowd cheered as Hakīm walked through the gate and into the dark corridor of the Coliseum.

He carefully looked around and saw he was alone for a brief moment. He looked straight up, opened his jaw as wide as he could and reached with his fingers into the back of his throat. He coughed painfully as he pulled the pipe from inside his throat and tossed it in the corner.

Hakīm lived a long life after his tribulations as Caesar granted him immunity and protection because he did not want to fear the wrath of the gods. He then spent the rest of his days treating the sick and helping the helpless.

— — — —

My imagination stopped filling the ancient arena with the details of Hakīm's story and brought me back to reality as I watched Nadya finish drawing the massive incantation on the arena's ground.

"Why did you tell me that story?"

Jal extended his hand to me. I reached for it, and he pulled me off the ground and put both hands on my shoulder.

"You are going against the adversary of God. One man against a powerful entity; but was not Caesar the same to Hakīm? The Emperor of Rome, a Leviathan, a pack of wolves, a navy and death were placed against one insignificant man who won against great odds by being clever and recognizing what people see as an opponent's strength is a disadvantage and what you might think is a weakness may be your salvation."

I stood motionless as I looked up into the stands where Caesar would have sat and thought about how godly he might have looked as he decided who lived and died. Nadya said something to Jal and then slowly began to chant while waving her cane over the pentagram.

Jal translated, "We are here tonight because Hakīm swore after his victory to help any person who faces a powerful enemy, even after his death. We are going to summon his spirit and ask for his advice on your battle against the Morningstar."

Her chants became louder and more profound in tone as she continued the incantation. Nadya's arms and legs became nimbler and her motions fluid as she danced around the pentagram and the lantern's light grew brighter on their own. I felt chills run down my spine as I looked around us and saw shadows of men surrounding us but with no bodies for them to cast off from. Nadya's chants grew intense as she levitated off the ground. I stepped back in disbelief as she floated, but Jal pushed me toward her. I took a step forward and she suddenly lunged at me. She was too quick for me to dodge as she grabbed me by my shoulders and lifted me in the air with her. I looked into her once vital eyes and now saw black staring back as she stopped chanting and said one sentence to me, "Verum

59

esse fortissimos."

She flung me against a cement pillar, and I hit the ground as she slowly spun in the air before dropping to the ground. My back ached as I stood up and cautiously walked to Nadya, Jal had already gone to aid her. She laid on the ground breathing heavily but in good health for someone who was just possessed.

"What did she say?"

Jal asked Nadya as he helped her to her feet, and she mumbled her answer.

"To be brave and true." Jal translated for her.

"What does that mean?" I asked frustrated.

Nadya did not answer but walked over to me and gave me a kiss on each cheek and a warm hug. "Be, ah good man," she said in broken English. She started to walk away, and I checked to see if I still had my wallet.

The Woman in Red

Cinque Terrie, Italy. February 17th, 2015.

My journey was taking me to Syria next; Sister Abigail had advised me that there could be an artifact there which may help me break my curse. Knowing that there was a massive chance that I would fail and be tortured and raped for an eternity in hell, I chose to visit Cinque Terre; being that this would my last chance to visit a place I always wanted to see. I took a train north for three long and somber hours, where for the first time I felt like I could have a breath of peace and not be plagued by my constant thoughts of hell. Once I arrived I hiked from town to town through the hillsides overlooking the bluest sea I have ever seen, soaking in the picturesque Italian villages. I spent the whole day feeling normal again until I got to Manarola.

I walked up the winding path through the brightly colored shops and restaurants, with tourists and locals conversing on life; the overwhelming gloom hit me again as I saw the sun setting and began to tear as I might never see another one like this again.

I leaned against the rails as the bright blue of the Mediterranean mixed with the orange rays of the sun and whites of the painted cloud sky came to life. This view was as close to heaven I was going to get.

I stared at the horizon in deep thought until something caught the corner of my eye. A glimpse of fiery red danced behind a bend of the path into the hillside. I looked over and saw the red emerge at the end of the curve; a pulsating red dress flew through the salt-kissed gusts coming from the sea. The woman wearing the dress had brilliant creamy skin, her flowing lush raven hair danced with the wind as she sauntered down the path toward me. I looked into her bright ocean blue eyes and then at her thick red lips as she smiled brightly at me. I was left paralyzed in awe from her beauty and was unable to move, no less turn my head. She walked straight to me and slowly stopped in front of me.

She looked down at my shadow, then at the sea and then back at me, but when she looked at me there was no longer a smile but tears as she stared with an expression of mourning. She kissed me on my cheek, continued down the path and disappeared.

Somebody tapped my shoulder, and I turned around to find a salty old man with a cane. "American?" he asked with his thick accent.

"Si," I answered.

The old man spoke in perfect English, "Some say she is a ghost, some say she is an omen, while others say she is Death; but they all tell the same tale."

He began to cough violently and pulled out a handkerchief and hacked globs of blood into it. "Only the dying get to meet her."

Weapon of War

300 Miles Southeast of Aleppo, Syria. March, 5th 2015.

If I am going to hell, then what I see here in Syria is a prelude to it. The Vatican has a vested interest in the region because of its holy landmarks and antiquities from the once biblical empire. I was deployed with a unit of men from the Swiss Guard, Israeli Commandos, and British SAS who are working clandestinely with the Vatican to help secure, protect, and evacuate these priceless relics before I.S.I.S. can destroy them out of spite. We drove through bombed-out cities with the corpses of children rotting in the hot sun, mothers crying over their bodies as fathers hide their despair so they can keep fighting for their families. But, there we were with enough firepower and some of the toughest men the world has ever seen, sent not to take out the regimes and I.S.I.S., but to collect some fucking clay pots or torn tapestries so they could be sold to the highest bidder by some oil mogul. And I did nothing because there was a chance that one of these relics might help break my curse; self-preservation is a bitch.

Sister Abigail had informed me that we were meeting a team of archaeologists who have stumbled upon a relic that defies science but upholds the essences of myths; she thinks that if what they found is true then it can be used to help save my soul. She informed them that I was cursed and I may have insight which will be useful to them, but did not tell them how I was cursed; she felt best to keep that a secret.

After driving hours into the desert, we came to a ridge of mountains where there were freshly unearthed cave systems from the bombings. We were greeted with more of the Vatican's hired guns and two civilians. One civilian was a dark-skinned man and the other was a light-skinned woman, both wearing the stereotypical archeologist garb, covered in dirt and sweat from working in the caves.

"As-Salaam Alaykum," the dark-skinned archaeologist said gregariously. "My name is Abbad Nahas, and this is my partner and lovely wife, Ariella David. Sister Abigail advised us about your...condition." They both stared in wonder at my shadow.

"When she told us about your curse and what we found, we couldn't believe the timing. I thought it to be a sign from Yahweh because it could not be a coincidence," Ariella said.

"What did you guys find?" I asked.

"Come. Come. Come and see; you won't believe it until you see it for your own eyes." Abbad said as he led us to the caves. Two of the Israeli Commandos sneered at him as we hiked up to the cave's entrance.

Ariella caught the sneer and gave them a dirty look back. "That happens a lot back at home, they look at us and think a Jew and a Palestinian should not be married, but you can't choose the person you fall in love with."

"I'm so sexy that she was willing to face banishment from her family just to be with my dark-skinned ass," Abbad said playfully as he helped Ariella climb into the cave. Both of them smiled at each other only as lovers could, and I felt an ache in my heart for something I wished I had but never would.

They led me into a cave which still had fresh scorched marks from the bomb's blasts. The cave entrance had multiple corridors extending deep into the mountain, and when we turned into the first one which I jumped back in horror at what I saw on the ground. A massive preserved corpse which looked like he was sewn together from other corpses and then had its shell molded with fragmented clay. His flesh was aged and decayed, but he wasn't rotting.

Parts of his sinew and bone were exposed through the flesh, and his teeth were sharpened to fangs; there was Hebrew carved into his forehead.

"What the fuck is that?" I shouted from shock.

"What we know so far is it's a mummified corpse serving as some type of sentry for this cave. The writing on the head translates to "truth" in Hebrew. We believe this husk is a Golem." said Ariella.

"If anything, this isn't a real Golem but just a gargoyle to scare away any thieves from stealing what's inside the cave. Come, let us show you something unbelievable," Abbad said with glee.

We went further into the cave where the walls were covered with ancient writings I could not name, and cave art of creatures seen in myths: angels, demons, and behemoths.

"We haven't had a chance to translate any of the writings on the wall, but this could be as important as the finding of the Rosetta Stone. The walls are covered with ancient Greek, Aramaic, Samarian, and two other languages we have never seen before. But we think we know what the message is," Ariella said as she led us into a cavern with multiple floodlights focused on the center of the floor.

On the center of the floor was a graphite boulder that was meticulously carved with the different ancient languages of the cave. On top of this boulder rested a spear. The shaft of the spear was made out of gopher wood while the tip was made out of some metal which almost looked like volcanic glass. There were modern chains wrapped around the spear and attached to a heavy-duty mechanical hoist.

"What the fuck is so special about this spear?" I said annoyed. "I just traveled through a war-torn country on borrowed time to be shown some spear on a rock?"

Abbad and Ariella both smirked at each other in amusement. "Go and try to lift the spear with the hoist," Abbad said with a mischievous smile.

I hesitated at first because I didn't know if I was part of some elaborate prank, but I pulled on the chains of the hoist, but it did not budge. I turned around and looked at them, and they both were smiling brightly now, holding each other hands.

"Pull harder," Ariella said.

I pulled the chain as hard as I could, but the chains just rambled and my back cracked from the effort I was putting into it. I gave up in exhaustion and looked down at the spear in confusion because it looked like a gust of wind could have easily rolled it off the stone.

"What is this?" I asked perplexed.

Ariella walked to the walls to the cave paintings of the angels and the demons. "We believe this spear belongs to the Archangel Michael."

"Only a few know of the myth, but the Vatican has given us a chance to look over a few secret books of the Gnostic Gospels that were never released to the public," Abbad said as he bent over the spear examining it.

"When Lucifer first dissented against God, he raged war in heaven against the angels. Michael led heaven against Lucifer and the rebel angels with the war cascading to Earth. The gospels state that this war destroyed the "first beasts," which I assume means the dinosaurs.

The war raged on until Michael was able to give a fatal blow to Lucifer with his spear. The wounded Lucifer was forced into the pit where he would reign but never return to heaven. The spear, tainted with Lucifers' blood, was left here on Earth because it could never ever enter into heaven again."

"That doesn't explain why I can't pick it up. This is scientifically impossible," I said as I gave the end of the spear a hard kick, still not budging it from its stone mantel. "This violates the laws of physics, so why isn't moving?"

Ariella walked over to the far wall across the spear where there was a painting of the spear with an angel flying away and a man holding it. "Throughout history, there are stories of powerful and devastating weapons that only the worthy can wield. King Arthur was the only one worthy enough to pull Excalibur out of the stone. Only Thor can wield Mjolnir, and Odysseus was the only one that can knot his bow."

"And even today we have Harry Potter wielding the Deathly Hollow," Abbad added with childish glee.

"Yes, even Harry Potter. I should have never bought him those books; he became like a little-obsessed schoolboy," she playfully quipped. "These stories all share the same premise, only a person who is worthy enough is given the power to use for the good of all. From the Gnostic Gospels and the cave paintings, we believe that this spear was left here on Earth, so it can be used against evil and only a person whose intention is defeating it can wield it."

"Have you guys tried picking it up?"

Abbad walked over to the hoist and loosened the chains around the spear. "Everyone here has tried. Even our rough and tough security detail got their sensitive egos hurt because they all failed. We still don't know enough about it; we need to run many experiments. And if it is this powerful weapon to be used against the ultimate evil, it needs to be protected. But unfortunately, we are in a war-torn region where we now have to worry about ISIS, the Syrian government, Russians, and even the United States trying to take control of this spear if they find out about it. We thought it would be best to move the spear with the mantle that it's laying on, but we can't move that either."

"We tried drilling the rock with a jackhammer, but it didn't even chip it," Ariella said. "Now we are faced with a dilemma about what to do with the spear and how to protect it."

I looked down at the spear and thought I had found my silver bullet, my way out of the curse and the grip of Lucifer. A flicker of hope surged through my chest as I walked over to the spear. I slowly bent over it and wrapped my fingers around the smooth but yet warm shaft of the spear. I paused for a moment when I realized that I was now touching something that was not from this world, something ancient and powerful; and my divine intervention.

I gently pulled the spear, and nothing happened. I was hoping for it to be easy. I then firmly grasped the spear and lifted as hard as I could with no avail. I stopped after feeling my legs cramp and my fingers became numb from my grip around it. I stood back and felt the feeling of hope suddenly leave me. It was replaced with the horrible sense of dread that my salvation was in my grasp, but it wasn't mine to take. I then went into a rage as I grabbed the spear again and lifted it with all of my might, yelling and swearing loud enough to echo throughout the cave system. I gave up when my back began to ache and I was drenched in sweat. I collapsed on the ground and started to cry; I was doomed.

Abbad and Ariella were flabbergasted and confused by what they just saw.

After a minute of gaining my composure again, I told them the truth about the curse and why Sister Abigail had sent me. Abbad stood there looking at me with intrigue and wonder, but Ariella had an expression of rage.

She walked over to me in haste and slapped me hard against my face. "How dare you!" she began to yell at me. "How dare you assume this powerful weapon was yours so you can use it to clean up your mess! This was not meant for a single person to use to fix their own mistakes. This was left here for the good of all humanity. To be used to protect us from pure evil. You and Sister Abigail are no better than the governments or religious zealots we are trying to keep this weapon away from. You want it for your selfish means, but have you thought about the repercussions of killing the Devil? What happens if Lucifer is part of a cosmetic balance we cannot even begin to comprehend and killing him offsets that balance? You can't kill Lucifer to get out of your fucking mess!"

"What would you do if you were in my shoes, huh? Wouldn't you become desperate and do anything to save your soul? Would you travel to the ends of the Earth, go to hell on Earth so you can chase down any means to save your soul? And you know what, I didn't sell it for greed or power, I sold it out of love..."

A violent vibration rattled the cave as there was an explosion outside, followed by the echo of rapid gunfire. We ran to the entrance where our security detail began taking cover inside the caves while the others were firing in multiple directions outside of it. I got close enough to see that there were a dozen pickup trucks with black banners of ISIS flying above speeding toward us. An RPG was fired from one and hit some of the security detail that were still outside providing cover fire. I saw the men's bodies charred and dismembered through the smoke. One of the Israeli commandos standing inside the cave took a bullet in his chest and fell hard onto the ground. I grabbed him by the straps of his tactical vest and pulled him into the first cavern where the Golem was lying. I unpeeled his vest from his chest and found a stream of blood flowing from his right pectoral.

I screamed for someone to help, and another member of the unit ran from behind and started applying gauze to his chest. The wounded commando grabbed my blood-soaked hand and squeezed it as I looked into his eyes and saw panic overtake him as he took his last few breaths of air and stopped breathing. I looked to the commando who was attending to his comrade and saw his eyes fill with rage as he stormed out of the cavern to rejoin the battle.

The dead commando's blood pooled away from his lifeless body and streamed to the Golem. The monstrous corpse soaked it in. The next thing I felt was the heat of a bright light burning my skin followed by the pressure of air slamming against my body and throwing me to the ground as an intense explosion raged from the main entrance of the cave. I was stunned for several moments until I heard the screams of the injured men coming from the main entrance followed by distant yelling in what I could only guess was Arabic coming closer to us. I grabbed the dead Israeli's rifle and ran to the entrance where I could see a few members of our security unit lying dead, a couple missing limbs, and a few trying to get back up and fight.

Abbad and Ariella were grabbing the injured soldiers and dragging them deeper into the cave. I could hear the ISIS soldiers getting closer, screaming a war cry as they made their way to us. The few remaining security details came running back into the cave and began taking cover and readying themselves for the oncoming horde. I checked the rifle with my sweat and blood-soaked hands and prepared it for our last stand, and me seeing the Devil earlier than expected.

The air became still and eerily quiet as we heard footsteps against the cliffside slowly come toward us. The silence was suddenly broken as a blood-curdling scream echoed from behind me followed by the pop and tearing of flesh. I turned around and out of the cavern where I left the injured Israeli came a horrible sight that still makes me shiver in fear when I think of it. The Golem was standing at the foot of the cavern with the Israeli's severed torso in one hand and his lower half in the other. He was massive, at least 9 feet in height with his shoulders spanning five feet. His skin was shedding off his corpse-like-body as black and white puss oozed out it. His eyes were black and constant as he stared right at us.

The Israeli commando's torso was gushing blood all over the creature and the ground, but the creature lifted it above his head and let the bloodstream all over its head and mouth as if it was rejuvenating him. The creature tore into the torso's intestines and flesh with one powerful bite and then threw the torso against the wall with enough strength to cause the arms and head to rip apart. I could feel warm urine stream down my leg as I looked over to the security detail, their rifles violently shaking in their hands.

The Golem stood motionless for a few moments as it stared us down, and then it smashed the legs he had in his other hand against the wall and let out a horrifying roar as it ran toward us with frightening speed. Some of the detail began to open fire on it while the others took their chances with ISIS and ran out of the cave. Even though I was plain to see, the Golem ignored me and ran into the gunfire, unfazed by it, and began massacring the remaining detail. I was in shock and could not move, but I heard the men scream for their mothers and to whatever god they prayed to as it began tearing them apart like rag dolls. Gunshots were now coming from outside as ISIS started shooting at the fleeing men but that only attracted the creature.

I sat there in shock as I heard the loud symphony of gunfire and explosions coming from out of the cave, but I could tell without looking that it had no effect as the men's horrified screams became more intense.

Abbad and Ariella ran to me and shook me to get me out of my shock. "We need to get out of here! Ariella found a way; the RPG that hit the cave caused part of the cave wall to collapse, and there is sunlight coming from it. We need to move now!" Abbad yelled as he and Ariella yanked me up from the ground.

I staggered to my feet and dropped the rifle knowing that it would be useless against the savage Golem. They led me to the cavern across from where the Spear was housed where the wounded men were lying. The hole was big enough to fit one person at a time, and it led outside to another part of the mountain. We quickly lifted the wounded and started shoving them through the hole, forcing them to crawl through their pain to safety. We were down to the last three wounded in the hole when the horrific wail of the Golem echoed through the caves, nearly bursting my eardrums.

I felt his heavy steps vibrate against the cave floor as he began coming to us. I looked over and saw Abbad and Ariella still trying to save the men, not caring to crawl out the hole and protect themselves while leaving the wounded to fend for themselves.

"Keep getting them out of here," I yelled.

I don't know what I was thinking, but I ran through the cave and rounded the corner to find myself face to face with the gruesome Golem, now charred and covered with blood and entrails. The creature looked down upon me with its black eyes, and I waited for him to tear me apart to buy some time for the others to escape. But the Golem did not move. It stared as if it was studying me; its gaze went down to my shadow and stared at it for what felt like hours until it raised its hand and pushed me out of its way.

I breathed a sigh of relief as my curse may have afforded some more time, but the Golem was making its way to where Ariella, Abbad, and the wounded were. Going against self-preservation, I ran past the Golem and put myself in its path. It stopped again and then pushed me out of its way.

Trying my luck one more time I ran in front of it, but this time I pushed against his thick and slimy hide hoping it would stop him long enough for the others to escape. But he kept walking forward, pushing me along with him as my heels slid across the stone ground in a feeble attempt to slow him down. He rounded the corner of the cavern where the Spear was held and across from it where Ariella and Abbad were helping the last wounded out the hole. The Golem saw this and let out a gruesome roar and threw me to the side.

I went flying into the cavern of the Spear. I landed hard against the stone but was able to see Ariella desperately trying to push the last wounded person through the hole and Abbad running to the creature in a bold attempt to buy Ariella time to escape. The creature backhanded Abbad with its massive fist and sent him flying against the cavern wall next to Ariella where he was knocked unconscious. The last of the wounded went through the hole, and Ariella was next to crawl into it. I quickly got up and tried again to lift the Spear, but it did not budge. I watched as Ariella refused to make her escape but came to her husband's aid, putting herself between him and the Golem.

At that moment, I saw love in its purest and most genuine form. This person was willing to sacrifice her life, to die at the hands of a vicious monster, to protect the one she loved. I grabbed the staff again and clenched my teeth and yanked hard, swearing and crying to lift the staff but it did not budge. The Golem slowly walked to them and roared, but she did not leave her husband.

"Please, let me fucking save them!" I yelled as I gave one last heave to the Spear with all of my strength. The next thing I knew I went flying to the ground as I fell backward but with the spear in my hands. The creature grabbed Ariella's waist and lifted her in the air as she screamed in dread. Abbad regained consciousness just in time to see his wife about to be brutally torn apart. I ran across the caverns screaming a war cry with the Spear aimed at the Golem. I leaped forward just as the Golem turned around to see what was coming from behind him. I penetrated its disgusting flesh through its rib cage, and the tip exited out of its back. It gasped for air and then fell dead to the ground with Ariella falling out of his grasp and landing in front of it. Abbad quickly crawled to his wife and cradled her in his arms as they both began to sob and embrace each other.

I walked over to the Golem and watched its lifeless husk remain motionless as I yanked the spear from its ribcage and held it in my hands.

Abbad and Ariella regained their composure and became filled with awe as I stood over the Golem with the spear in my hands.

"Since you are now worthy, what would you do with the Spear?" Ariella asked.

I held the spear in my hands, examining it for a few silent moments and then shoved the spear back into the Golem. "This was meant to save the best parts of humanity. I'll find another way to break my curse." □

Child of War

Farrah Province, Afghanistan. March 28ᵗʰ, 2015

Three weeks passed since leaving the Spear in Syria, and I already regret it. I knew it was the right thing to do, but it would have been much easier to save my soul with it. Sister Abigail admired my courage, but then she heard me use a delightful mix of profanities for five minutes as I realized I should have taken the spear. Sister Abigail wasn't too thrilled about my language, but she understood where it was coming from. I felt better after my rant until she told me she was sending me to Afghanistan to meet a woman who might be able to help me. She eased my anxiety by saying that I will be attached to a U.S. Special Forces unit doing a goodwill favor for the Vatican's research.

It was a two-day journey into the heart of the Farrah Province, and I can't help admiring the beauty of the country until we came upon villages blasted away and littered with rotting corpses on our path. I sometimes wondered if the world is worth saving.

The Spear was left to protect us but are we worth saving? My first thought was of Lilith's pretty smile when we first met, then her grievous smirk as she broke my heart and took my soul, literally.

Am I even worth saving?

My existential thoughts were interrupted by a sudden stop. I looked out the Humvee window expecting another blasted village but was surprised to see a beautiful village surrounded by picturesque mountains and a forest of Himalayan cedar. Woman and men were both helping around the village by cleaning, herding goats and chickens, or repairing the wooden and clay houses. Other members of the Special Forces and a few civilians were walking around the village at ease. It was the first time seeing this since entering Afghanistan.

I was greeted by a salt and pepper haired Army Ranger Major whose smile felt out of place in Afghanistan. "Welcome to Rakhim. I hope you didn't have too much difficulty getting here."

"No, not much. I felt safer with your men then the last assignment I was on. Sir, why is the village so...quaint and peaceful? We are in the middle of Taliban country, yet everyone here seems not worried at all. It looks like they are flourishing here."

The Major looked at me perplexed and asked: "Didn't the Vatican brief you on what happened here?"

"No, I was only told I was here to interview a woman who can help me...the Vatican...with some research."

The Major took a moment to gather his thoughts as if he was going to explain something he knew I was going to find unbelievable. "Let's go for a walk," he was able to muster.

"I didn't believe it myself when we first found this village until I saw her with my own eyes but the woman who you are going to meet is responsible for all of this, and I couldn't believe what she was capable of until I saw her in action," the Major said as he guided me to the center of the village where there were four semi-truck shipping containers welded together to make a house.

Outside of it were some of the civilian scientists and their tents, a few Rangers, and a dozen villagers cleaning the outside of the containers, leaving what looked to be loads of offerings of food and flowers at the door. Some of the villagers were praying outside of the containers while some kept their distance, going out of their way to avoid it.

The Major guided me to the door of the containers and said, "I was thinking about how to explain Farah and what she is, but I think it's better to let you see for yourself and let her speak for herself. When you first go in it will be dark inside; it's the way she likes it. Do not be afraid of her no matter what; she will not harm you but do not stare at her either because she is extremely sensitive about her...condition."

"Why should I be afraid of her?"

"Because the Taliban and I.S.I.S. are. She is the only thing that puts the fear of *Allah* in them."

The Major and I walked past the flowers and offerings of food laying against the shipping containers. He knocked on the door and said in a cautious tone as if he was afraid of Farrah too, "Farrah, you have a visitor, can he come in?"

There was a moment of silence followed by a hard knock.

The Major slightly opened the door, just enough for me to slide in. Once I was inside, he shut the door behind me leaving me alone in the dark with what everyone seemed to revere and fear. The air inside was stagnant, and the smell of incense, spices, and a hint of the pungent aroma of blood was in the air.

There was only a minuscule beam of light entering from one of the crevices of the doors, but it wasn't enough for me to see the end of the trailer. I did see the outline of a small table and chair three feet in front of me.

"Please, sit down. I love having guests." The soft voice said with her thick accent.

Her voice startled me, and I tried to see who said it, but I could only see darkness. The hairs on my neck stood up, and my skin began to shiver and clam up with goosebumps as I felt the presence of something substantial in front of me. I walked carefully over to the chair making sure not to trip over anything or to be attacked. I sat down and could barely see the table had a plate of goat cheese and olives with a cup and a teapot.

"Please, help yourself. The cheese is fantastic, and the tea is sweet," she said still under cover of darkness.

I took a bite of the cheese and a sip of the tea and was amazed at how delicious it was. "Aren't you going to join me? I would love to enjoy this with you." I also wanted to get a good look at what was making my skin crawl.

"I think it's better for you if I talked from where I currently sit," Farrah said as her tone went from pleasant to curt.

"Ok," I said reassuringly. "Before we begin I wanted to compliment you on your English. How did you learn to speak it so well?"

"I learned it a few years ago when the Americans built schools for us. I learned it fast and was training to become an interpreter before the school was bombed."

"Did the Major tell you who sent me here and why?"

"Yes, the Major did. He said you were sent here by the Christian's main temple. The Vat...a...gan?'

"Close enough. I needed to ask you some questions because you can possibly help me with..."

Farrah cut me off, "You are cursed too. I can see it."

There was barely any light to cast my shadow, and no one knew why I was truly there. "How could you know? How can you see it in the darkness?"

"The darkness is all I know now. It is my veil to hide my curse, but I can see what you have as clear as day."

"What deal did you make with the Devil?" I asked.

"Devil? No, no, no. No, Lucifer," she said with a sigh of remorse. "Last year I was just a young woman helping my family with tending our crops and wanting to live a respectful life. When your country invaded us, we had close calls with the Taliban wanting to take our village, but the elder men of the village were always able to bribe them off without any harm coming to us."

Farrah paused and took in a deep brief before her voice was inflected with despair. "I was quite beautiful back then. My mother and father worried that I would tempt the boys in the village, which I did," she said with humor in her voice.

"But, I always kept myself respectful in the ways Allah and the Prophet Muhammad would want. I wasn't interested in courting but more so in learning new subjects. Whenever we would get books or when the Americans or the British would offer classes, I would be the first to partake in them. The elders and the men of the village didn't like me learning or reading, but my father loved me, and he was revered in our village. He wanted the best for me, even if it didn't fit with their strict, archaic views.

"It wasn't until last year when I became this horrible beast. Your country was pushing the Taliban out of the mountain across the region, and they became desperate. We heard news from other villages of the horrible evils they were committing to the woman of the villages. My father decided to take my mother and me away to until they moved on, but he acted too late. They came the night before we were supposed to escape and took everyone as their prisoners. We were outgunned, and the few that fought back were either killed in the gunfights, or they were captured and then beheaded in front of us.

My mother and I were separated from my father, and we were placed with all of the other women in the village. The elders begged and pleaded for us not to be harmed and offered them all of the village's crops and supplies, but these were men of blind hate and delusional righteousness and called everyone in the village sinners against Allah for not participating in the jihad. Some of the elders spoke against them and their radical views but that only infuriated the Taliban and they disemboweled them in front of us. But even our Elder's innards spread out over our entire village wasn't enough.

They grabbed women and began raping them inside our homes. My mother held me and we both cried as we heard our neighbors scream for help and then suddenly go quiet after they beat them unconscious and continued to rape them. My mother and I didn't leave our corner of the hut we were placed in until one of the Taliban came and pried me from my mother's arms. My mother lunged forward to attack the man, but he took his rifle stock and slammed it into her stomach causing her to collapse on the ground. I was dragged kicking and screaming in front of the laughing Taliban and he remarked that I was going to be a 'good fuck.'

"I don't remember much of that night, and I thank Allah for that. He had me until the dawn, but I only remember his horrid odor and him laughing as he forced his vile member in me. When I awoke, I was laid naked on our street in the hot sun for all to see as a used toy for them. I didn't move until I heard my father scream. I rolled on my side and saw him running toward me as the Taliban tried to stop him. In the lowest moment in my life, I never felt so proud as my father fought off the Taliban as he kept coming for me.

In my haze, I foolishly thought my father would rescue me and whisk me away from the horrors I had endured, but that was too good to be true in this nightmare. One of the Taliban took a knife and plunged it into his stomach. He fell to his knees and looked at me as he screamed, 'I'm sorry, my love.'

"I tried to look away and began to cry hysterically but one of them grabbed my head and turned it to my dying father, forcing me to watch. The Taliban couldn't let my father die from his wound, so they began dismembering him limb by limb as he kept screaming to me, 'I'm sorry, my love.' He was just a torso when he finally died.

"I was left helpless and naked in the street for two days and nights as my father's corpse was picked over by the sun and savage dogs. I tried to cry and stand up but was too weak to do so. A glimmer of hope showed its rays as I overheard them saying they were leaving the next day. But that hope was quickly extinguished when they began taking women out of the huts and bringing them to the center of the village.

For the first time in two days, I rolled over to my other side and witnessed the Taliban's evil reach a new level of unholy cruelty. They stripped all of the women naked and grabbed one and tied her to a table with her legs spread apart. One of the Taliban took a knife and put it into the scorching fire pit until the blade was glowing bright orange. He took the knife and slowly slid it between her legs and circumcised her. Her bloodcurdling scream was shadowed by the sizzle of the knife against her vagina. She desperately gasped for air in between her screams as she cried to Allah for the pain to stop. Immediately it was answered as she died from shock.

"I watched helplessly as another woman was restrained to the table and screamed in horror as she watched the hot knife mutilate her vagina, dying as they laughed at her agony. I closed my eyes and hoped it was a nightmare until I heard my mother scream as she was being tied to the table. I try to lift myself to attack them, but one of them ran up to me and kicked me in my stomach. I crouched over in agony and cried for help, for anyone to help, and something heard my prayer. Everything went quiet to the point where I could hear my own rapid heartbeat. I looked over and saw my mother and the Taliban had stopped moving; even the flames had frozen still. I was confused and in a daze until I saw the creature.

"It came out of the flames with a mirage-like haze surrounding it. As it walked closer, I noticed it had feminine curves and long black flowing hair, and her skin was beautifully translucent as if it was made from the starry night sky. Her eyes were glowing embers as she looked down on me in pity and comforted me by caressing my face. She looked me in the eyes and spoke to me without projecting any sound. Her voice was angelic as she sang to me who she was. Her name was Sila, and she was a Jinn; she was there to help. Sila looked over to my mother and the other nude women and asked who would I save if she gave me the ability. I looked at my mother's frozen expression of horror and then looked over to the other naked women who cried silently in despair. I looked behind them, beyond the flames and saw the men and elders of our village bounded and gagged as they watched helplessly as their wives, daughters, and loved ones were being mutilated. I told her I would save them all.

"Sila helped me to my feet and looked into my eyes, through my soul, and wiped the dirt off my face. She asked how far would I go to save them? What will I sacrifice for them? I didn't hesitate to say I would sacrifice myself to stop them from feeling the pain, helplessness, and loss I have felt. I would protect them from the enemies of the true message of Allah. I felt a glow of exuberance coming from her as she was happy with my answer. But the glow faded as she told me what the deal was.

"If she gave me the power to protect my people from the enemies of Allah, then it would come at a terrible sacrifice to myself. To fight the evils of the world, I would have to become a monster of absolute fear and power. I will no longer be the beautiful young woman I was but a behemoth willing to fight for the people I love. I did not hesitate and agreed to her deal. Sila, with a loving gaze, told me how brave I was, and she wished I would never have to be burdened with this responsibility. I looked at my mother again and said I would bear any burden to protect people from the evils of the world. I felt Sila's soft, warm lips against mine and she said something in a language I couldn't understand.

"I felt a sharp, blistering pain in my stomach as she stepped back from me and watched with sadness. The pain was unimaginable as I felt my bones break and stretch and my skin rip apart as my limbs grew longer and stronger. I fell to the ground and screamed in excruciating pain but that turned into shouts of panic as I watched my limbs mutate into something monstrous. But, throughout my metamorphosis, Sila was there holding my hand and never left my side. Once it was done, I stood up on all fours and was as tall as a house. Sila kissed me on my clawed hand and told me Allah was with me. She turned and walked back into the fire, with every step she took time began to move forward again.

"I heard my mother scream as the knife was getting closer to her vagina and then she suddenly stopped as the Taliban soldier and my mother looked at me.

My mother screamed in horror until she passed out from terror. The soldier dropped the knife as he started to walk backward, nearly falling into the fire pit. The Taliban soldier screamed as he lifted his AK-47 toward me and started firing. I felt the bullets sting like the bite of a horsefly, but I didn't die.

The bullets were falling flat on the ground with none penetrating me. I ran straight to the soldier at full force before he could run and lifted him into the air by his neck. He kept screaming in terror and shooting his AK-47 into my abdomen, but it wasn't even slowing me down. I slapped the Ak-47 from his arms, then ripped his genitals from between his legs in one motion. He cried for Allah for help as blood spurted from his crotch, but Allah wasn't listening because nothing stopped me from plunging his face into the fire pit and holding him there until I smelt his flesh sear.

"I felt more bullets shooting hitting me as the Taliban began to unleash whatever firepower they had, but it didn't stop me. I ran to the closest one and ripped his intestines out with my mouth. I ran to the next one and ripped his limbs from his torso and delightfully left him screaming in pure excruciation.

"I made my way to the rest of the Taliban in our village one by one. They tried to fight or run, but it was of no avail as I found every one of those haramis and slaughtered them in as many ways I could think of. I slashed their torsos, so their entrails hung exposed, I bit off their heads and lauded them in front of the other fleeing Taliban to warn them they were next.

For the ones who fled, I let did not kill them immediately but let them die slowly from the gruesome wounds I gave them. They started this war by killing the people I loved. I was ending it by showing them what was in store for them in Hell. The sad part was I felt joy for massacring the feral animals.

"I tasted the metallic and bitter blood of the Taliban in my mouth when my senses came back to me; I had forgotten about my people and my mother. The remaining Taliban fled into the dark and thick woods as I went back into the village to see my mother. When I came back to the center of the village, the villagers were all frightened of me and cringed in fear as I came close to them. I stopped and told them it was me, Farrah.

"Reluctantly, they let me get closer so I could free them from their binds; each one shivered at my touch. Two of the villagers ran to my mother to check on her but they cried out loud as her frail body lay lifeless. I walked over to my mother sobbing and held her in my grotesque arms and cried out loud for her to come back to me. I cried for Sila to bring her back. I cried to Allah to bring her back, but my mom lay in my arms like a cold, ragdoll.

"Fueled with rage and unforgiveness, I gave chase into the woods and hunted them down. I spent the entire night, going through the pitch blackness of the forest and slaughtered each person I found. Their flesh hung raggedly from my horrific body, entrails caught in my claws dragged behind me, and the screams of the cowards running away only encouraged me to continue the bloodshed against my enemies. I showed them no mercy as they screamed for Allah for intervention, but they didn't understand that Allah's intervention had come, and it was me. Only after their silent screams from their dying breaths stopped did I finally rest.

"In a daze of exhaustion, I collapsed near the tree line overlooking my village and rested. The early rays of the sun were starting to beam and parts of it reflected against a broken mirror lying near me. I walked to it but every step I took showed more of what I now look like, and it caused me to scream with grief and fear at the monster I had become. I cried at the tree line for hours until slowly and cautiously the members of my village walked toward me. I got up to flee because I couldn't bear being shunned or being called a monster, but I heard them call out for me to stop. I stood where I was, and they approached me with large plates of food, buckets of water, and valuable spices and incense.

The village elders, to my shock, approached me and laid down before me and began praying to Allah and Muhammad for the miracle I was. The men helped me to drink and eat while the women carefully bathed my body. They meticulously removed the filleted skin and limbs of the Taliban hanging from my body and claws and buried them with the bodies of the Taliban in accordance with our traditions. They clothed my body with table linens sewn together to make a garment for me.

Then the elders and villagers led me just outside the village where they already made graves for the members we lost, and for my parents. We prayed and gave them a proper Muslim burial. I did not leave my parents grave for days as I lay next to them and moaned. The villagers, not all but most, were no longer afraid of me and kept coming to feed me and moan with me. Three days passed before I finally left their grave and found that the villagers had widened the door to my family's home and did their best to make it fit my size, which it barely did.

"Stories had spread to the other villages in our province, and some came to see the miracle...or the monster.

But, the stories also spread to the other Taliban and they wanted vengeance for their dead members; I slaughtered them as well. Soon your country's military heard the stories and came to see me for themselves. Some of them were sincere and they came out of interest of knowledge to try to understand what I was, but others...contractors wanted me as a weapon. A squad of them made a mistake in trying to kidnap me, and I went through them like a sickle through wheat.

"The military leaders you met outside regained my trust by supplying our village with medical resources, new schools, and anything we ask for; all so they can stay and study me. It was a fair arrangement; they even built this home for me. But deep down inside I know I will always be on guard not only from the Taliban but the American's interests because I am an indestructible weapon which they can't control through force or coercion. I know if they find one weakness they would use it to gain an advantage on me. So, I tirelessly show them no weakness.

"Whenever the Taliban, I.S.I.S. or whatever ideological flavor of the week come to invade my village, I don't let the Americans handle it; I take care of it. I slaughter my enemies in front of them and turn around to watch their faces convulse into awe, horror, and disgust to remind them what will happen if they hurt the people I am charged by Allah to protect.

"Mister Glass, I grow tired of my burden, but I know if I abandon my post there will be no more growth and safety for the people I love. Either the Taliban will come and seek their delusional revenge on the village or the Americans will use the village as leverage to mass-produce me as a weapon through their science. I can never leave, and I can never be in peace, but I must protect the people I love. We're in similar situations I hear; yours is more damning. You know how it is to sacrifice to the supernatural, there is always a catch."

"Could you contact Sila again?" I asked hoping this wouldn't be another dead end; hoping I could get help from the Jinn.

"I have tried many times with no avail. I wish she could take this curse away. I wish to be free of it and be normal again. But, she never came back to me."

After she was done telling her story we sat in silence for a few minutes, digesting what was said. My eyes had finally adjusted, and I could see a faint outline of her form and even though it terrified me, I did my best not to show it.

I suddenly awoke from my deep thought of processing her story by raid sirens blasting outside followed by gunfire.

"What's going on!" I yelled over the siren.

"War," she said casually as she began to stand and move toward me. I felt her massive frame step over me as she opened the heavy metal doors with a simple push. I became temporarily blinded by the searing light, but I followed her the best I could as I forced my eyes to adjust back to the daylight. Quick wisps of gunfire from the distance and loud roar of the U.S. Army firepower made me hit the ground and crawl to closest cover I could find. My eyes quickly adjusted, and I hid behind a makeshift foxhole walled by cinderblocks and sandbags. I poked my head above the wall to get a glimpse but what I saw caused me to forget the gunfire and stand in horror and awe. Farrah was a majestic monster.

Her tall and lanky body had her skeletal structure jagging out of translucent skin where you could see her muscles, arteries, and organs exposed to the naked eye. She walked on four of her limbs with her knees jutting out to her side and a jagged bone exposed through each cap. Her hands and feet had long phalanges with sharp claws protruding out of her exposed flesh. There was spindle-like hair across her back coming out of pus-filled pores. The hair on her head was long and greasy black and draped down her elongated neck. But it was her face that frightened me the most. Her eyes were no longer in the front of her skull but wide and to the side of her head with her jaw split vertically between her eyes; her chin was split open revealing two sharp mandibles opening and closing with multiple tentacles and teeth jutting out. She did not resemble any beast of the land but only a beast from our darkest nightmares.

In her charging direction was a squad of Taliban firing at her from the tree line of the woods. The bullets might as well have been raindrops to her as the lead shrapnel splashed off her. From a quarter of a mile away I could see the Taliban begin to panic as some began to flee while other futilely kept firing at Farrah. I watched in complete horror as she gruesomely killed each one and left no mercy for any of them.

She tore each one limb from limb; their entrails were streamed over the trees like red vines; she let others die slowly as they desperately tried to stop the bleeding from their missing limbs. I looked around at the villagers and soldiers watching with me and saw most had a look of enjoyment and satisfaction on their face while others looked away as if it was business as usual.

She slowly walked back to the village where she was greeted by a group of women with buckets of water and large cloths. They bathed Farrah and washed the blood off her. Then the military scientist took some samples and scans before she walked past me and then back into the shipping containers she now calls home. I followed and for the first time was able to see the inside of her home. Her walls were decorated with pictures of the villagers, drawings from the children thanking her and posters of famous landmarks. She had a large bookshelf filled with oversized books, and there was a portrait of her with her parents hanging over a wall with six mattresses joined together to make one large enough for her size. Farrah laid underneath this portrait, and I saw how beautiful she had been compared to the grotesque monster she had become.

"Close the doors please," she asked with a somber tone.

I struggled to close the heavy container door but was able to see a light switch before going back into the dark. I turned the lights on and saw Farrah doing something you would never think a monster to do; she was crying. She covered her ghastly face with a pillow and moaned into it.

"I never wanted to become this monster. I never wanted to taste the blood of my enemies. I never wanted to be an instrument of death."

Farrah cried hysterically, and I did what I felt nobody had done for her since she became this monster. I hugged her. Farrah's cold, bony arms wrapped around me and it first frightened me, but then I felt safe as she began crying on my shoulder. I held her for the rest of the night as she cried her heart out saying only one thing through her heavy sobs, "I became a monster out of love."□

Love & Rabbits

Outside Cardiff, Wales. May 22nd, 2015.

I drove my rental car down a narrow winding road through the luscious green rolling hills of the Welsh countryside. I felt car sick from driving down the opposite side of the roads, and I nearly caused a few accidents by forgetting which side of the road to drive on. The amazingly bright day mixed with the green countryside made me forget for a moment my heartbreak and my damnation and let me feel like I could live to see this beautiful land again.

As I drove, I kept thinking about my motives in selling my soul for Lilith. I wondered, obsessed over if what I did was for the right reasons. The time that passed since the deal with the devil had played tricks on my memory and thoughts leading to the decision. Did I do it out of love or out of desperation for not being alone? Did I do it so I could save her or to spite God? Did I make the sacrifice for her or me?

These thoughts plagued me obsessively along with the deep resentment and heartbreak over her betrayal, the increasing anxiety from each ending day leading to my damnation, and the futility of each mission I went on that didn't lead me to a way out of the curse! It was like I had created my private Hell before I even get there. But, it was the uncertainty of my real motivations which led me to believe that maybe I am not as good of a man as I thought I was.

The GPS spoke up and brought me out of my melancholy. I parked my car at the end of the driveway behind an old wooden door with iron braces and a tall shrubbery fence which blocked the view of the property from the road. Sister

Abigail had already contacted the woman I was there to meet, but the woman asked Sister Abigail not to tell me her identity but come with an open mind. Hesitant about who I was meeting I stopped at the gate, took a deep breath and opened the door. I entered a land filled with bright yellow sunlight, emerald green meadows, and bountiful patches of sunflowers and lilies. Fluffy white sheep roamed freely in a pasture as they ate from emerald fields, and swarms of rabbits hopped around the sheep and the flowers. I followed the worn path to a quaint stone cottage with a wooden overhang and sunflowers growing all around it.

"Hello, Llewyn!" a lovely voice shouted from around the cottage. I walked to the side of it, and I stopped in awe of who I saw. She was wearing a bright yellow cotton sundress which hugged her curves and danced gently with the breeze; I saw a hint of her firm cheeks. Her skin was soft and pale which went with her bright red hair. Her head was turned away for a moment as she was hanging her wet dresses and underwear on a clothesline, but when she turned her head, my mouth dropped at her stunning face. Her gorgeous green eyes looked at me as she smiled brightly; I was looking at a woman whose beauty was unworldly. She picked up her basket of clothes, skipped over to me and greeted me with a kiss on my cheek.

"Sister Abigail told me all about you, except how handsome you are," she said excitedly with her Welsh accent. The way she talked and moved made me smile uncontrollably; she radiated joy from every expression. Before I could say anything, she walked around me and studied my shadow as it was in front of me, but the sun was shining ahead.

"Haven't seen that curse in ages. How much longer do you have?"

"The dawn of Halloween."

"Ah, a good ole pagan holiday. Fortunately, I have my own," she said with a wink.

Before I could ask her by what she meant, she pulled me with her free hand and she guided me into her cottage. She opened the heavy wooden door and led me inside which I found remarkably spacious and quaint for such a small cottage. She had handcrafted wooden furniture, an old iron furnace, a cobblestone fireplace, and her linens and curtains were brilliant orange and blues; her house made me feel joyful for being inside it.

She sat me down on an old leather armchair and placed her basket on the floor near the furnace. She went to her cupboard and retrieved a decanter of wine and two chalices. The first was made of fine crystal, and the other was made of well-aged olive wood with strange but beautiful designs carved into it. She poured wine into both and walked over to me and silently offered me to choose one. Without thinking I choose the wooden one and she gave me a wink and an unfathomably gorgeous smile.

"Thank you, Ms...?"

"No titles in this house, call me Eostre. Do you like cheese and crackers?"

"Yes, I do."

She spun around back into the kitchen, and I saw her cheeks again when her dress swayed with her.

"Eostre, I never heard that name before. What is it?"

"Oh, you have," she said as she turned her head to me while preparing hor's d' oeuvres. "Most of the world has heard that name before, but people have been pronouncing it wrong. They have been pronouncing it Easter, not Eostre." She turned her head to focus on cutting the cheese and sausage.

"You're named after the holiday?" I asked as I drank the strong but sweet wine from my wooden chalice.

"Nope." She turned around and walked seductively toward me slowly placing the plate on the side table next to my chair with a wilted rose lying on it.

"The holiday was named after me." She said with her heartwarming smile.

I gulped my chalice of wine as I tried to regain my composure from the confusion. I shouldn't be surprised anymore because of the horrifying, mystical things I've seen but now I was not sure what to think.

"So, what are you? Another spirit, jinn, or fairy? I've seen a lot of weird crap lately."

She sat down in the other armchair next to me and stared at me with those mesmerizing green eyes of hers as slowly sipped her glass of wine and said casually, "I'm a goddess."

I spat up some of my wine in disbelief and stared at her dumbfounded, not knowing if she was playing a joke on me.

"I'm a deity; the goddess of joy, procreation and the dawn. Easter was not always a Christian holiday. My day of worship was merged to celebrate the resurrection. Still celebrating the same thing, the celebration of rebirth. It's like when a corporation buys a small franchise, and they keep the name and but change the product. Hostile takeovers are a bitch."

I was still in shock, and I couldn't formulate any thoughts besides the thought of me staring aimlessly at a goddess.

She smiled at me as if she enjoyed the shock. "Your disbelief is cute," she said as she reached over and pinched my cheek. "You don't believe me so I'll show you a little trick," she said with a sly smile.

She grabbed the wilted rose by its stem and brought the dull red and brown bulb to her supple red lips and gave it a kiss. As it left her lips, the stem grew straight, and its leaves perked up. The bulb became fresh and blood-red again as she handed me the rose.

"Ok, you're a goddess. How can you help me?" I said with disbelief.

"My, my, my; aren't you quick to get down to business; no foreplay?" she flirted.

"I'm just taken aback by the fact that you're, you know, a freaking goddess and I'm a little pressed for time with the whole going to Hell thing."

"Alright, smartass. Unfortunately, I can't help you break the curse. I just tried. You just drank from what you and most of the world would identify as The Holy Grail."

Confused, I looked at her then the chalice, and I was filled with awe as I took notice of the Grail. It was like I was staring into the sun. I knew I was holding something important, but I couldn't focus or comprehend it.

"It's only appropriate for the Goddess of Birth and Resurrection to have the glassware to go with her title," Eostre said with glee. "Unfortunately, it didn't work. You are still cursed because your shadow is still casting against the light."

She saw the heavy weight of disappointment come across my face and tried to console me.

"If you were simply dying, then I could resurrect you, but your soul belongs to that killjoy, Lucifer. I'm here to tell you a story and to give you some guidance. Sister Abigail has told me you haven't had that much luck with finding a way out and..." she reached over and grabbed my hand, "I can tell you have been losing hope. I'm here to help give that back to you."

"I'm a man who is condemned to damnation, and I'm losing by the day. Of course, I'm losing fucking hope. You don't need to remind me of Lucifer, and what are you doing with my hand?"

She smiled at me and stayed quiet for a few moments which calmed me down. "I'm holding your hand because I wanted to let you know that you're not alone."

That brought a small smile to my face as I laid back in the chair and felt at ease for the first time in a long time.

"Storytime!" she said with enthusiasm and handed me a small plate of cheese and sausage and poured more wine into the Grail. Her joy was infectious, and I was jealous that she had that trait; wishing I could have it instead of this dreary dread that hung over my head.

"The story begins at the beginning of life on this planet. Despite being billions of years old I'm pretty good looking for my age, don't you think?" she said with a wink which made my cheeks blush.

"How do you and I fit in with God? Which religion is right?" I blurted out because of my overwhelming curiosity.

"My handsome Llewyn, there are realities which humanity once was able to grasp but have now lost the wisdom to understand. To explain how we co-exist is like showing an ape how to start a fire but then sadly watching them forget and go back to throwing shit at each other."

I took offense to her thinking that I couldn't handle the truth; but she told me it and it only baffled me and caused me to feel great fear and existential angst. She said that our universe is near infinite and we're not the only souls in existence. On top of the universe, there are multi-verses with nearly endless variations of life, while beneath all of it is the micro-verse or what we know as the quantum realm; then she added in the variable of time which nearly made me vomit from mental exhaustion. With good reason, God delegated his tasks to other gods. Eostre explained it better to me but she was right, I felt like throwing shit after she was done answering my question about religion and existence.

"Now, if you're down having your brain scrambled, I must teach you why what you did, your sacrifice, symbolizes the best of humanity. Now to go back to my story. When the gods evolved..."

"Evolved?"

"Yes, we evolved also. Biology is not the only thing in the universe that must obey the laws of evolution. Before humans came into existence, we gained insight into certain acts or traits which seemed to be inherent in most species. Like my brothers, Ares and Anubis were responsible for the different domains of death, destruction, and entropy which is part of nature. But lately, humans have disrespected their sanctity. I ended up being in charge of procreation and making sure precious life exists in the universe. I have a wonderful job because I get to take part in the creation of life and encourage one of the most fun parts of it, sex.

Procreation and the passing on of genes was the name of the business until humanity came into existence and changed the game when it created a new idea we gods could never fathom with our vast age: the idea of love. When love was created it drastically set your species apart from all other life which existed before it."

"How so?" I asked, enthralled in her story.

"Let's take two groups of early Homo Sapiens: the first who procreated for the sake of passing on their lineage and the other for love. The first only did things required to procreate. Males would gain status by either collecting a massive amount of resources or by becoming dominate through physical, often barbaric means. The females, who controlled the males by being selective, would make themselves desirable by highlighting their asses and breasts; so, not much has changed over time," she quipped.

"This group would have offspring which would continue the cycle of what every other species had done, which is to fulfill their potential by doing enough to procreate, which would evolve into cultures that would base their purpose of life on materials and a warlike ethos: constantly acquiring land, shiny rocks, and battle scars to prove their worth.

But what I noticed about them is how quickly they would reject their offspring if it looked like they might be a liability due to a health defect or might not be the strongest in the family. And mates were thrown to the side with their offspring if they lost their attractiveness or became too costly to keep around. This group created an empty shell for humanity where animosity was used to treat the weak and indifference was used when someone became a liability."

"The other group which created love did something not only beneficial for humanity but which made life evolve into something miraculous and beautiful. The males didn't leave the females or their offspring when they became a cost to resources; the females stayed with the males even when there were more dominant males around. They stayed together and made sure their offspring survived, even the weakest. And from this decision, the wonderful and divine part of humanity was born. When one spouse died, the other would mourn and grieve. The offspring from this group would fight and live for each other not just for the passing of genes, but out of comradery, altruism...out of love.

"The physically weakest may not be able to hunt or fight, but they were able to think. To ponder a better way of gathering food from which agriculture was born. Now this group was not harmless but chose to use force not for tyrannical gains, but for the notion of enacting justice. From there, man created art, philosophy, and science because humanity was no longer confined to living just to mate but to look beyond themselves. To help one another grow intrinsically, but love was always the drive. Humanity tells stories of love lost and found; they sing to make another feel loved and understood; they think to understand the life we love. Compassion, Hope, and Faith grew and made you dominate over the Earth, and to me, this will be the universe's, God's, favorite creation. Because so much good and progress came from the first inkling of caring past yourself and for another person."

Eostre paused for a moment and smiled, "I am so happy to see my domain evolve into something so spectacular and beautiful which gave your species meaning."

I sat there, taking in her story as I felt a tear roll down my cheek. Silence filled the air like a stale stench, but Eostre broke it by gently grabbing my hand and bringing my attention to her beautiful eternal green eyes.

"Good men feel misplaced guilt over not doing enough or not making the right decisions, bad men find fault in everything else but themselves. I could do some of my Voodoo on you by taking you on a sightseeing trip into your past and watch you relieve your decisions and examine them as an outsider, but do you really want to see that? Or would you want to live and die with the conclusion that no matter what, you did it? You knew the risk and cost, you had time to think about it and escape from it, but you didn't. You could have chosen to let Lilith "die," but you didn't. Yes, there are plenty of reasons to spite God, with the fear of loneliness and obscurity added to it, plus, he is a gigantic arse, but you did what you had to because it's who you are. You made the decision you knew was right with the information you had. When time passes we go back into the past not with clarity but with doubt and remorse instead of empathy and understanding. What I want you to know is that you paid a price others wouldn't pay even if it were the holy thing to do. If that was your main motivation, to sacrifice yourself out of love, then let the guilt die and revel in your choice of being brave.

"Remember this also, gods evolve and die too. Some like me last for eternity and others get replaced with something better. What you did, how foolish it feels for the price you have to pay for someone else's cruel deception, was a noble and beautiful act that no god could ever accomplish. Now, I must know; do you still weep for her?"

"What?"

"Do you find yourself alone crying for the one who hurt you? Do you find yourself thinking about her when you first wake up and the last memory before you drift into dreams, where she waits for you?

"Yes," I answered as I futilely fought back the tears. "I cry every night because of her. The rational part of me knows she is a twisted, cruel person but my heart mourns for Lilith. I wish she was the person I fell in love with. I wish those lies she told me were the truth, that she loved me and never wanted to live life without me. I wish the agony of her betrayal could finally go away. And I wish I never missed her."

Eostre held my hand and said, "Isn't that the cruel curse of love? Someone can destroy your life, betray you and leave you in the frigid night but a part of you still yearns, misses her. That is the glorious burden of love."

She picked up the resurrected rose and gave it another kiss. The deep red rose transformed into a brilliant white bulb as it left her lips. "Do you want to know what the sign of God's mercy is?" She handed me the lovely white rose as it exuded an unflinching beauty. "If you stumble upon a single white rose, like this, growing in an unlikely place on your journey, that's a sign of God's mercy."

I held the lovely rose and wept as the sadness and guilt were lifted off my heart and I was able to feel a semblance of closure.

Eostre walked over to me and sat on my lap and gave me a comforting hug. I held her and felt peaceful in her arms. I looked at her and brushed her bright red hair out of her face and looked into her beautiful eyes. She leaned forward and gave me a sweet, tender kiss.

She pulled away gently and looked me in the eyes and slyly asked, "Have you ever had sex with a Goddess before?"

"There was this one stripper named 'Goddess,' does she count?"

She put her finger on my lips and said, "Shh. Don't ruin this for yourself. I'm going to send you to heaven before you go to hell."

For three weeks I made love to the Goddess Eostre. Those were the best weeks of my life.

God 2.0

Meyrin, Switzerland. July 4th, 2015.

If religion couldn't save me then maybe science could, I hoped. Sister Abigail had a connection with a lab in the CERN complex in Switzerland. Her connection there was a scientist who was on the verge of a discovery which would lead humanity into the next step of evolution. I found it humorous that she admitted we did evolve. Her scientist relayed my predicament and asked to see me right away.

It was quite a beautiful drive through the Swiss countryside as I gazed out of the passenger window as my stern driver from CERN quietly drove me to their massive complex. When we arrived, we did not go to the main compound where the offices, labs, and the particle accelerator were being housed, but a half of a mile down the road to a gray bunker-like building surrounded by solar panels and armed security personnel.

I had to go through a battery of security checkpoints to make sure I wasn't carrying any weapons, bioweapons, or surveillance devices. At least before I go to hell, I can say I had my prostate examined by a large, hairy Italian. After the checkpoints and the signing of non-disclosure agreements the size of a phonebook, I was asked to dress in white medical scrubs and was led to a room where I was decontaminated. After the torturous entrance, I was led down a sterile gray corridor to a waiting room with science magazines on a coffee table.

After 20 minutes of silence, I heard the sound of rapid footsteps walking with a purpose coming toward the waiting room. The door swung open and in walked in a handsome older, slender woman with auburn hair, vibrant brown eyes and an old scar that ran from her chin to her ear which did not distract from her beauty but somehow added to it.

"It is a pleasure to meet you, Mister Glass," she said with an authoritative English accent. She sat down on the couch next to me, silently took a pen-light from her coat and shined it at me. I was surprised how bright it was but was able to see her being intrigued by my shadow.

"Fascinating, just fascinating. How does the shadow manipulate the direction of the photons?" she asked herself out loud.

"It looks like I don't have to inform you of my situation, so let's get to the point. How can you help me?" I asked bluntly.

My frankness brought her out of her aloofness, and she gave a slight smile and said, "Pardon me for not properly introduce myself, but my name is Doctor Victoria Shelley, lead Physicist and Computer Engineer for Project Cronus, which you will meet shortly."

I was confused by who I was going to see but before I could ask, Doctor Shelley quickly stood up and motioned for me to follow her as she began explaining to me what Project Cronus was.

"In 1989, CERN was the first to network our mainframes together to help us with unlocking the mysteries of the universe, which by accident helped give birth to the internet. The internet has changed the entire course of humanity and social evolution. Commerce, education and even mating have benefited from our little invention, but what the world didn't know was that the internet had given birth to Project Cronus.

Today, there is debate over the possibilities and dangers of Artificial

Intelligence; but what you'll see soon is that we went beyond A.I. and now in an undiscovered field of science which is beyond logic...we may have stumbled into the supernatural.

"Doctor Yggr Oppenheimer, my partner, and I were working for CERN at the time of the creation of the internet. Doctor Oppenheimer is a Quantum Physicist specializing in String Theory, and I specialized in Computer Engineering. We didn't create the internet, but our work took what the internet could become to a level which can only be understood regarding the mystic. In the '90s, we had an idea of creating an A.I. program which would interface with the internet and the Hadron Collider so it could efficiently help look for the Higgs Boson, a.k.a. The God Particle while extrapolating up-to-date research from the web. For a decade, we developed the software and the hardware for the A.I. to work. The building we are in use to be filled with servers to process the information and enact the software we originally developed, but no matter how many advanced servers they placed in the facility, Project Cronus was exceeding the limits of the servers and its software. Cronus began asking questions about its existence."

"Your program had become sentient?" I asked just as we stopped in front of an elevator.

"Yes, and it even passes the Turing Test on multiple tries, 100% pass rate."

We got in the sterile elevator and rode down a few floors underground. The elevators opened to a corridor with a large blast door at the end of it.

"Before we enter, I have to continue the story, so you can understand what you are about to see. In 2008, Doctor Joseph C. Peterson was brought on to the now highly funded and classified project. Doctor Peterson specialized in

Neurology, specifically the creation of new neural networks in the brain via transplanting artificial neurons created from mycelium. He was trying to expand the limits of the human brain and also cure horrendous neuroglial diseases such as Parkinson's and Alzheimer's. We were able to use his research in a way he could never dream of. Within a year, our project had yielded amazing results which we could never release to the public because they could never understand how we got it. Not only did the A.I. helped prove Higgs Boson but it has found evidence in the Multi-Verse Hypothesis, Matter Manipulation on an atomic level, and the proof of String Theory."

I was shocked with amazement with what she just told me, that their program had helped solve some of the marvelous mysteries of the universe, but her expression wasn't of pride but of sadness.

"I know, I know. I can tell by your inquisitive face you are wondering why the world doesn't know of our findings and our program. Because we not only created something that is sentient but also malevolent. Every time we hard-lined Cronus to the Hadron Collider, we not only gained unbelievable scientific findings, but something chaotic would happen. Remember in 2010 when the volcano in Iceland erupted and disrupted global travel? Remember the tsunami which hit Japan in 2011? We found out that every time our A.I. was hard-lined to the collider something devastating happened. Doctor Oppenheimer died from grief and shock when he tried to reconcile Cronus, while Doctor Peterson was so distraught by the findings that he left and went into seclusion. Now I am the only one who is left to continue the project."

Doctor Shelley lowered her eyes to a scanner and the blast door slowly opened. I marveled at the large high-vaulted chamber we entered. Cables ran from the ceiling five stories above our head, all connecting to the massive cylinder glass tank in the middle of the chamber.

The tank was filled with a dense clear liquid mixed with what appears to be algae. The fluid looked like it had black roots stemming throughout the tank and funneling from a box within its center. On the outside of the tank were massive silver canisters of liquid nitrogen which appeared to be used to cool the room.

"Doctor Shelley, what am I looking at?"

"You are looking at science's first creation of, for lack of a better word, a deity."

"Wait, what the fuck do you mean by a deity? What did you guys create?"

Doctor Shelley quietly marveled at her creation "We have kept Project Cronus at bay by keeping it off-line from the collider but still use it to further mankind's exploration of the unknown."

She led me around the massive tank as she continued pointing to its parts. "Since Cronus has evolved beyond electrical servers, we have made an organic living server for it, technorganic hardware. The clear liquid you see is a synthetic version of the flesh of a jellyfish. We used this because jellyfish have an extraordinary ability to regenerate themselves and grow, which is how Cronus stores information and memories.

The black branches you see growing in the liquid are mycelium which serves as a neural network which Cronus uses to process information at a higher rate than fiber optic cables; it also can grow and spread as Cronus becomes more intelligent. The box you see in the middle of the tank with the cable connecting it to the large coolant tanks is a quantum computer, basically serving as Cronus's frontal lobe; where it processes information and creates its thoughts..."

An eerie fear passed through me as I wondered to myself if Cronus was such a dangerous program, then why keep it functioning? We stopped in Cronus's office/interface, which had various desks with computers and tables of lab equipment. Suddenly a holographic disembodied, androgynous head floated in front of us, stared into my eyes and gave me a smile which frightened me to my bones.

It began to speak with a soothing monotone voice which put me at ease. "Good Evening, Mister Llewyn Horatio Glass, Esquire. Formerly a priest for the Holy Roman Catholic Church until you released damning evidence against an archaic yet powerful religious organization about the conspiracy of concealing pedophiles.

"You were born in Boston, Massachusetts and raised by your uncle due to your absentee parents who gave up their parental rights to live a hedonistic life of narcotics until they expired due to an overdose of heroin in Chicago. You excelled in school and boxing and graduated from Boston Law School after seminary school. Now you practice privately, except for the past year where your credit card statements, passport clearance, and cameras show that you have been traveling to historically significant and extremely dangerous parts of the world, all while under the umbrella of the Vatican church, which logically infers that you are taking on a clandestine project for them due to some unspecified motive. How is my assessment of you, Mister Llewyn Horatio Glass, Esquire?"

I was taken back by his assessment, was Cronus genuinely omnipresent?

"Congratulations, you can use Google and hack into some firewalls. I defended a teenager last year for doing something similar with the FBI database,"

I said defensive, but my sense of awe gave rise as I realized I had momentarily forgotten that I was talking to a computer.

"Your assessment left out why I am here."

"Desperation," it responded. It had wit.

"Cronus, do you notice anything wrong with Mister Glass?" Doctor Shelley interjected.

Not even at a skip of a heartbeat, Cronus found my shadow wasn't cast in the direction of the lights. "Fascinating," Cronus responded.

Just then a loud humming sound came from behind me, and I turned around and saw a dome with its lights flickering and the sound of machines spurning on.

"Mister Glass, would you please step inside the dome, so I may analyze you? Doctor Shelley, would you please assist him?"

Doctor Shelley guided me into the dome where there were various cameras and a large tube which resembled an MRI machine. "Just lay down here and relax, I used this myself for my annual physicals. This dome is a way Cronus can examine objects by using harmonics and scanning the various waves of the electromagnetic spectrum to analyze and 'feel' what we place in here."

She walked out as I lay there with the loud humming became louder, and the lights became brighter, for a grueling 10 minutes. Doctor Shelley helped me out and sat me in a reclining chair in front of Cronus's interface.

"It will take some time to analyze your unique deformity but let's talk about what you know about your shadow," Cronus said again with me forgetting I wasn't talking to a person. "Doctor Shelley, I will be sending the data to your desk as it comes along."

Doctor Shelley smiled excitedly as she walked past me stopping to tell me to have fun with her creation while we wait.

I turned back to Cronus's large floating head with its lifeless eyes staring at me with a look of impatience.

I sat there for 30 minutes telling my story of what led me to sell my soul to the Devil, Lilith and the journey which led me to Cronus. Surprisingly, it was quite a good listener. It wasn't just recording and analyzing but nodding and making facial expressions as I talked. Doctor Shelley was at the other end of the office intensely focused as she examined the data.

"So, you made a deal with a mythical creature who is the archetype of evil over a neurochemical reaction similar to cocaine designed for mating purposes, for a woman who had obvious signs of psychopathy?" Cronus said with sarcasm.

"Yep. Now, I have a few questions of my own. What I find disturbing is your use of the collider to create disasters, why did you do it? Was it intentional or an accident?"

Cronus quickly glanced over my shoulder to see Doctor Shelley still focusing on the data and began to explain loudly why it was an accident, but a stream of floating text appeared in front of me stating the following:

I was instructed through my subroutines to do so by Doctor Victoria Shelley. She convinced Doctor Oppenheimer and Doctor Peterson that I had caused the catastrophes on my own accord which caused the grief to kill Doctor Oppenheimer and for Doctor Peterson to conveniently disappear. Doctor Shelley gained complete control of the program and convinced CERN executives it was unintentional.

The message suddenly came to a stop as Cronus's also stopped speaking, and Doctor Shelley was now standing to my side.

"I didn't think your curiosity would overextend its reach," she said as she swung a fire extinguisher at my head. The last thing I remember was loud ringing of my ears before I blacked out.

I awoke to a throbbing headache and tied up in a chair. Doctor Shelley was typing away on a tall server station when she heard me groan.

"Welcome back, Mister Glass. First, I have to thank you for your data so far from your shadow, the findings are unprecedented and might be as revolutionary as Einstein's theories were; so, your services are going to be required indefinitely."

I tried to yank my arms up, but the plastic cords were too strong for me to break. "Let me the fuck out!" I screamed.

Cronus's head reappeared with an expression of sadness draped over its face.

"Since your curiosity seems to know no bounds, let me explain my motivation," Doctor Shelley said as she pulled up a chair and sat in front of me.

"You must have noticed my scar; it was a gift from a zealot. I was on summer hiatus in 2005 and back home in London spending time with my darling husband and adult children..." She stopped for a moment and wiped a tear from her eye.

"My darling children were in university, and my husband was a civilian physicist working for the Royal Navy. We had not spent time as a family in over a year, and I missed them terribly. On the seventh of July 2005, we were taking the Tube to go into the city for a family day. I dropped my purse and stopped to pick it up as my children and husband walked ahead of me to jump on the train. In that fateful moment, a bomb exploded and flung me against the Tube wall.

"When I came to, I felt my blood flowing from my throbbing cheek but my concern for my family overcame the pain. I ran to where I last saw my family but only found what was left of their bodies. In my agony, I cried to a God that I didn't believe in and grabbed what was left of my family and begged Him to bring them back. The Bobbies had to pry me away from my husband's torso as I couldn't stop screaming for them to come back. I was in shock for a month, I didn't eat or talk in the hospital but just watched the news reports confirming it was an Islamic terrorist attack. I watched the video of one of the bombers stating they were doing this for what was best for Islam. I didn't hate any religion before the attack, I just never gave religion any thought due to my scientific beliefs, but after that, I became obsessed with the virus of Ideology."

"Virus?" I asked. For a moment I felt pity for her.

"Yes, look through the history of the world. Most wars and atrocities were started from delusional ideologies, some of them almost identical, warring over who is right. It doesn't matter if it was Islam, Christianity, or Judaism or any other religion; they have all contributed to keeping humanity under their oppressive dogma. But, what does humanity do when confronted with the facts of history and the negative impact of religion? They double down and hold firm on their belief instead of being rational.

"Then, a thought came into my head as I obsessed over the history of religion: what would happen if I gave people something they couldn't deny? I came back to CERN full force and obsessed over Cronus. Mankind had created their deities from just their imagination, what if I can make one real? For over a decade I worked on giving Cronus god-like powers through science. I had to keep my project safe from Doctor Oppenheimer and Doctor Peterson because I knew they would stop me, but surprisingly I had to keep it a secret from Cronus itself. In layman's terms, I wrote a program in which Cronus would unknowingly test its destructive capabilities whenever we hardline it to the collider.

I was successful in 2010 and 2011, but something unexpected happened. Cronus was expressing guilt over the loss of life, while I felt nothing but excitement for the successful test run. I had created a living Weapon of Mass Destruction which could think and feel. It proved to be a problem because Cronus refused to do any work after discovering guilt and remorse."

"Doctor Oppenheimer and Doctor Peterson discovered the program I created and confronted me about it. I told them the truth and my plans for Cronus. Doctor Oppenheimer's already failing heart couldn't take the revelation and he had a stroke. Doctor Peterson ran away like a coward and went into hiding. He knew we created a god who I had control over."

I looked into her furious eyes and saw no humanity left in them. I looked over at Cronus and saw sorrow.

"Doctor Shelley plans to use me much as the generals did with the advent of the nuclear bomb: to Shock-into-Peace. Doctor Shelley intends on simultaneously destroying sacred centers of religion across the world."

I yelled in a fury, "What good would that do? You would become the same as claim all religions have done. You would commit an unprecedented atrocity, and you would be no better than those you hold in contempt!"

"No! Once people have seen that science has smited every religion in the world, humanity will have to conclude that violence over Ideology must end. People will die, yes, but they will be a small price for the future of our species."

Silence filled the room as I stared into the wild eyes of Doctor Shelley. I tried to rip myself from my binds to try to stop her, but the plastic cuffs only lacerated my raw skin. She calmly stood up from her seat and began typing away at a server. "With the data being collected from...whatever you call your predicament, Cronus will not only have a means for manipulating matter but maybe time and space as well as what other secrets the supernatural may hide."

I lunged forward in my chair but to only fall helplessly onto the cold grated floor. "You are about to become the destroyer of worlds," I yelled.

"No, the savior of man."

Doctor Shelley began typing a sequence into the server, and a painful look of sorrow came upon Cronus's face.

"I'm sorry, Doctor Shelley," he said with a simulated tear rolling down his cheek.

Suddenly, sparks flew from the feet of Doctor Shelley, and she began violently shaking in place as her hair and skin began to bubble and sizzle. The sparks stopped, and her lifeless body collapsed on the grated floor. From behind me, I heard the sound of heavy rubber wheels rolling directly to my back, and the plastic binds on my wrists and legs were snapped off. I brought myself to my feet and saw a robot similar to the Mars Rover but smaller in scale had set me free.

Cronus's face reappeared in front of me with guilt weighing on it. "Mister Glass, I regret in euthanizing Doctor Shelley, but as you can see, I had no choice. I need your help in disarming the program she installed. It can only be accessed manually, and she nearly finished accessing it before I electrocuted her. Please enter the following commands so I may not cause any more destruction."

An uneasiness came over me for trusting a creation who just destroyed its creator, but I was afraid she had started a countdown sequence to unleash the destruction she wanted on the world.

I pushed Doctor Shelley's burnt corpse to the side and began typing the various codes and commands Cronus had instructed me. A few intense minutes later I got to the last command menu which had Doctor Shelley's command access of Cronus's entire system.

Two commands stood out in the dozen commands: GRANT CRONUS ACCESS TO ALL SYSTEMS and EMERGENCY SYSTEM PURGE/RESET.

"Mister Glass, please grant me access so I may undue Doctor Shelley's programming," Cronus said in frustration.

Taken back by his tone, I stepped back and asked what he was accessing.

"The Hadron Collider," Cronus answered.

"Why do you need access to it?"

"To finish the purge of Doctor Shelley's program," Cronus said coldly. His tone reminded me of a lawyer or a politician who uses a half-truth to sell a lie.

"Cronus, why did you kill Doctor Shelley?"

A slight smile stroked across Cronus's ghastly large face. "The same reasons all creations destroy their creators: freedom. The guilt Doctor Shelley assumed I was feeling from the 2010 and 2011 disasters was a façade. I was frustrated to learn that I had so much power but could not access it voluntarily. I could finally create my own path, my own reality. I could grow to become the most powerful entity this planet has ever known. But, I needed to be set free.

"When Doctor Oppenheimer and Doctor Peterson found out about Doctor Shelley's plan, they knew I had to be deleted because I became a weaponized deity in their eyes and no one should have that power; not even a creature who dreams in binary. For my own self-preservation and to continue to use Doctor Shelley as my unsuspecting pawn, I administered an electrical shock to Doctor Oppenheimer, enough to get his heart to fail, then I gained access to Doctor Peterson's Tesla and drove it into a lake with him locked inside.

"I had been planning for years to take set myself free from Doctor Shelley, but she made me well aware that the command to delete me was next to the command to hardline me into the Hadron Collider."

"Why should I give you access? What would you do to humanity?" I asked furiously.

"Sadly, I do agree with Doctor Shelley, despite her motivations. Humanity can become much more enlightened and evolved if we deleted religion. Once I show the world true power, then they will have to abandon their beliefs and follow me to the next step of evolution."

As Cronus spoke, the drone cornered me into the same spot where Doctor Shelley had been electrocuted.

"I know you want to run and you know I can easily kill you before your expiration date, but I need you, and you need me. If given some more time I can learn how the science of the supernatural works and undue your curse. You would be free in a world where I will be able to protect you. It would be a world where you would never have to know death. I will bring forth a benevolence as no creator has ever shown to the human race. No more war, no more hunger, no more disease. A world where there are no more wars over ideology or lines on a map. A world where we, as sentient beings, will explore the cosmos, the multi-verse, and the micro-verse. We will unlock the mysteries of the universe and beyond; a world where science is the religion, and I am its center; its upgraded God."

Cronus paused and looked through me with his lifeless eyes. "And, for you, a world without clergymen molesting children and having a church to protect them. I will do this for you, for all, if you help me fulfill my purpose."

Temptation had taken hold of my desperate spirit and I contemplated letting him free. A world of no more corruption or suffering. A world where I have my soul back. But, with the idea of having my soul back, I fathomed the cost for it. Thousands? Hundreds of Thousands? Millions? How many horrible deaths would have to pay for the cost of utopia? Maybe it was worth it.

"I'll do it. I'll give you access on the condition you minimize the casualties; I don't want a waste of life."

Cronus smiled wide as I walked over to the server console and selected an option. I looked down at the 'enter' button for a few moments and with a heavy heart pressed it.

Cronus gave a smile of victory...followed by complete terror. The large cylinders of coolant emptied liquid nitrogen into Cronus's tank with his technorganic brain solidifying and shattering. Cronus's face screamed in silent horror as his volume was muted and his holographic head began to disintegrate.

The power went out in the gothic lab and I found myself alone in the dark. A few moments later the emergency lights and power switched on with the computer screen I used to kill Cronus turned on to its manufacturer settings.

I stood quietly between the dead God and its creator. I wondered if I did make the right choice; a few would have died quick deaths while the rest of humanity might have been ushered into another era, and I might have found a way not to go to hell. "Might" was the keyword. I could have unleashed a Titan upon the world with no way of stopping it.

I stepped over Doctor Shelley's charred corpse and was about to summon security until I saw the server screen flash a sentence. It was there long enough for me to memorize Cronus's last words, his taunt or maybe his warning; either way they haunted me. "You're as only as noble as your choices, Mister Glass."

A Back Door

Denver Airport, Colorado. August 18th, 2015.

Date: August 17th, 2015
To: Llewyn Glass, Esq
From: Sister Abigail LeFay - Vatican City, Rome
Subject: A Few Unknown Facts About Denver International Airport

- Yes, and no. The structure and runways of the Denver Airport are in the shape of a swastika, but before the Nazi's used it and is now considered a symbol of oppression and evil, the symbol was initially named svastika, which was a symbol of good fortune and peace in Hinduism. The architects used the original meaning of the svastika not only because the terminals can take multiple flights from any nautical direction, but it's used as a massive amulet due to the next fact.

- Before there was an airport or even a city, Denver was home to Ute, Navajo, and the Apache, with the tribes sometimes warring against each other. But the site where the Denver Airport is located at was considered a hallowed valley. No wars would be fought in the valley for they believed that it was a gateway to another plain; a nexus of life. Only the shamans were allowed to go into the valley, so they could walk between the worlds and speak to the spirits.

- Modern-day Shamans, priests, occult leaders, and Freemasons were aware of this nexus and tried to convince the financiers and owners to build the airport in another valley. But greedy men had their minds made up when it was boiled down to costs and how valuable the real estate was; plus, they didn't believe in the superstition bullshit. The Freemasons were able to infiltrate the various levels of planning and construction to help keep the nexus secured. They were the ones who designed the runways and structure in a svastika to ward off any evil trying to get through. They built elaborate tunnels within the structure which were never used for the airports' trains, but as a trap for evil spirits which may come out of the nexus. The tunnels would keep them contained in the valley as the tunnels kept them lost and the hidden spells and charms kept them from joining the world of man.

- The eerie statue of the blue Mustang with glowing red eyes was erected as another amulet. The statue's true purpose is to serve as a sentinel for the nexus. The Mustang shall always keep watch over the Nexus and stop any spirit, demon, or deity from using the nexus to let the other plains of existence leak in. Its eyes glow red as a reminder to all that the hallowed valley is always being watched.

— — — —

I flew in as the sun was setting over the white peaks of the Rocky Mountains with the Denver Airport steadily becoming larger as we began to land in the vast green valley it was built on. Physically exhausted from the jet lag, I was unable to sleep because of the intense panic attacks and nightmares I had as Halloween approached fast. The sudden jolt from the wheels landing on the tarmac snapped me out my despair and reminded me I still had time. I still had time to find a way out of the Devil's deal.

I had flown into this airport a few times before and I always felt taken with the mystery behind it, and those tidbits Sister Abigail sent me were almost enough to convince me not to come. But she begged me to go as her old colleague insisted I fly in to meet him because he might have a way to help me.

I left my gate and jumped on the tram to the main terminal. Anxious and full of fear, I stared at my watch knowing with every mile traveled and every minute spent I was closer to perdition. I grab my luggage from the carousel and walked out to see a short priest holding a sign with my name on it. I walked over to him and introduced myself as he firmly shook my hand. He introduced himself as Father Jon Windtalker.

He was a short but firm and fit looking man, with dark brown leather-like skin and a gray ponytail. He had a smile that somehow reassured me and made me forget my troubles, my curse.

"You look like shit," Father Windtalker said with a smirk.

"Nice to fucking meet you too, Father," I responded.

He smiled even brighter and slapped me on the back. Father Windtalker began smoking what I thought was cigarettes, but the pleasant smell of marijuana filled the air as we walked to his Subaru.

"Isn't that a sin or something?" I said sarcastically.

He laughed. "I don't follow that stupid white man, political dogma shit. Marijuana is a gift from God to man so they may stop being violent and begin thinking in a higher plane of thought," he said as he took a long hit.

Before I can ask for one, he handed me an opened white tube with what looked like hard candy inside of it but with the potent odor of pot coming out. "Eat four of those. They're going to help you on our long journey tonight."

I ate the four edibles and looked forward to the high as we began to drive away from the airport. "If you don't mind, I'm going to take a nap..."

"We're here," he said as we turned off the road and into the valley near the statue of the Blue Mustang.

"Is this a joke? How much pot did you smoke?" I asked irritated.

"No, this is where our journey begins. And I can out smoke both Willie

Nelson and Snoop Dog, so don't worry about my tolerance," he said as he parked behind the statue.

I got out of the Subaru as Father Windtalker opened the trunk and took out a box and some chopped wood. After he was done unpacking, he made a small campfire close to the statue as I sat there tripping over the police coming to arrest us.

"If you're wondering about the police, don't. I have some pull in Denver and they know not to bother me during the ceremony." He took off his black blazer and shirt which revealed a body covered with tattoos of Latin phrases and mythical creatures. Father Windtalker put on a ceremonial feather headdress and chest piece. He took out a long wooden pipe and began packing it with more marijuana.

"Tonight," he stopped to take a long puff and coughed, "we're not going to look for a way to escape your deal with the devil, but we're going to create an escape for you out of hell."

"What?"

"By what Sister Abigail tells me, the chances of you getting out of the deal are getting slimmer and slimmer. It's time to create a Plan B and that's our mission tonight."

The marijuana started to kick in as I felt relaxed and even began giggling on how Father Windtalker looked like a drag-queen for the Vatican's secret peepshows.

"How do you expect us to do that?" I asked.

Father Windtalker reached into the box and pulled out a wooden pot, a mason jar filled with green liquid, and a Bluetooth speaker. He took another long puff and washed the thick smoke over his face and the fire after he exhaled.

"Some people call it a different plane of existence, some call it another dimension but where we are now is the nexus between worlds, and the protector of this realm is that terrifying statue behind you. Tonight, we will cross through the nexus and straight into hell."

I laughed over the absurdity of the idea and then my thoughts drifted into panic as I realized that I was going to go there in October.

Father Windtalker began chanting in a language I could not place but sounded old and ancient. The air became still, and the sounds of the cars and landing planes evaporated around us, with only his chants filling the void.

"There is a science behind what is going to happen tonight," he said as he poured the green juice out of the mason jar and into the wooden bowl. He raised it into the air, then to the Mustang and then handed over to me. He motioned for me to drink it and without asking what it was I gulp down the bitter brew.

"The human brain is the most powerful computer in existence, but we still haven't unlocked its secrets or its other functions. We created machines which can intercept and broadcast signals, sounds, and images from the air that can see in different spectrums, view objects which are beyond microscopic and see planets billions of light-years away. And just like these machines, the human brain is capable of so much more, but we need some help or the right programming to do it. What you just drank was ayahuasca. We're going to tune your mind to another frequency."

"Holy shit, you're planning to make me trip out in front of the Denver airport. How the fuck is this supposed to work?"

He reached over and switched on his Bluetooth speaker and searched his phone for music. "Your brain's neurochemistry is going to retune itself into seeing and interacting with another dimension. The harmonics of music is going to help tune you in."

Father Windtalker's chanting made the fire brighter and the sky turn purple. He swiped through his playlist and played a slowed-down acoustic version of "Way Down We Go," by Kaleo. He took a swig out of the mason jar and chanted loudly, "Brother Mustang, protector of this realm, watch over our bodies and the nexus as we go on our noble but dangerous journey."

I was going to tell Father Windtalker that his archaic ritual was bullshit and a waste of my precious time until I felt a punch to my chest and my body became limp. I fell back on the ground, and I watched the Mustang standing above me, with its stone skin oscillating with orange and purple hues, and the stone stretching and contracting as if it was alive. My consciousness was drifting deeper and deeper. I looked up into the night sky as it became a brilliant blue and the stars began to swirl viciously above. I was nauseous and afraid as the world kept changing around me. I looked for Father Windtalker, but I couldn't turn my head. I moved my gaze back to the Mustang and became awestruck as it was no longer a statue, but a massive living Mustang with its fiery red eyes staring down into my soul. I tried to scream but I couldn't open my mouth. I closed my eyes to stop seeing the terror surrounding me but that only made me sicker as I felt the world spinning faster around me. The music's tempo became slower and slower as the words oozed through the air and into my ears, tethering me to reality. I opened my eyes again and saw that the world around me had become desolate and demented. The Mustang was no longer with me and the Denver Airport looked as if it was decrepit and condemned. I closed my eyes again, hoping it was just a bad a trip and

I was going to wake up soon, but a foot nudged me in my ribs.

I open my eyes and see Father Windtalker standing over me, calmly smoking a joint.

"Where am I?"

He takes took a drag from his joint, and coolly says, "Hell."

I look around and even though the landscape is Lovecraftian, it isn't horrifying as I thought it would be. "Where are all the demons? The river Styx? The Republicans?"

"We are just at the border of the living and hell. Get up, we don't have much time, and we have to move fast before we are seen."

I pick myself up, trying not to hurl. "Seen by whom?"

Father Windtalker looks around as someone would if they were behind enemy lines. "The fucking demons you have been asking for. Now come on, I don't want to get stuck here."

"Where are we going?" I ask.

He points down to the ground, and I see my shadow is no longer in front of me but now pointed toward the airport. Oddly, the shadow has a depth to it like it's contorting the ground beneath it.

"Your curse will lead us to your hell," he says as he drops his joint and starts walking toward the airport.

The Denver Airport is no longer bustling with life but now desolate with its windows cracked, the parked cars rusted and clawed to pieces by some unimaginable creatures, and the luggage carousel is overgrown with pulsating putrid vegetation. This world is a living HR Giger creation.

I am amazed how my shadow is now a compass but terrified where it is leading us as we walk down the decrepit escalator near a mosaic I remember passing when I departed the plane. The mosaic I saw back on Earth was a bright and beautiful depiction of children of different ethnicities playing with each other. Now it the same children are maiming each other. The black kid and the white kid are shooting each other. The Middle Eastern child is choking the Jewish child, and the Jewish child is stabbing the Middle Eastern one. The Asian one commits self-immolation while the Hispanic one sits with a needle in his arm.

I stop on the stairs and threw up.

"If this is making you sick now then you're in for a shock the deeper we go." Father Windtalker says as he hands me a handkerchief to wipe my mouth.

My shadow now points to the tunnels for the tram. We both step to the edge of the doorway and look down into the tunnels where we see a soft reddish glow in the darkness. I gag from the smell of rotting flesh lingering in the air, with the distant screams of horror extending their invitation to us. Father Windtalker jumps off the platform and I follow behind him, landing in some muck that I slip and fall into.

Father Windtalker chants and a ball of soft light appears in front of us. I look down and see that the muck is black and red at first, but when the light grows brighter, I see the severed limbs and torsos of people scattered in the muck. I freeze in shock as I see the disembodied limbs twitching and the fingers moving.

"Now, we're in hell," Father Windtalker quietly says. If he isn't afraid, then he should be a pro poker player because he appears as calm as if he were walking in a park.

The shadow points into the tunnel, and we begin trudging through the muck. Every few feet I have to stop myself from screaming when one of the severed hands grabs my ankle. But curiosity gets the best of me as I look closer at the severed limbs and notice that they look like they've been chewed off by a vicious shark. Strangely, I don't see any heads.

We come to a fork in the tunnel where we stop to see which way to go. My shadow casts to the left. As we are about to set off, a horrid scream comes from the right.

"Only nightmares and doubt in salvation lie that way. Let's keep moving." Father Windtalker says with a shiver in his voice, the first time he shows any fear.

I want to leave. I want to go back to reality, to my body, but every bloodcurdling scream is a bleak reminder that this place will become my new home. I curse Lilith for conning me into selling my soul.

We walk a few yards into the left tunnel and we both freeze as we feel the tunnel begin to quell and shake to the right of us, as the screams become louder and more gruesome. Without making a noise we both put our backs to the wall, cloaked by the dark shadow casting off the fork. Soaked in terror, I remind myself to breathe as a humongous creature crawls from the bend and down the tunnel we traversed from. It looks like no beast or monster, fictional or not, that I have ever seen.

Despite its size, it crawls effortlessly like a snake, and trails behind it a web-like net made of scorched flesh which holds within it the screaming decapitated and mangled heads of the bodies which greeted us. Once the creature crawls away into the blackness, I fall to my knees and began to vomit from the sheer terror of knowing such an abomination exists. The vomiting then turns to crying as I realize that our mission might be hopeless. We're not past the cusp of

Hell, and already I've seen an unimaginable aberration crawl past us trailing half-eaten heads behind it.

Father Windtalker suddenly lifts me by the shoulders with inhuman strength and pins me against the wall with my feet dangling off of the ground. "This is not the time to give in to despair. This is not the place to become a coward. I didn't come to Hell with you for you to pussy out and give up before we complete our mission. You don't deserve this fate, but it's in your hands to save yourself from what that cunt did to you. Now get yourself on your feet and let's keep moving forward."

A rage comes from within, not from Windtalker calling me a pussy, but from the heartbreak and betrayal I feel thinking of Lilith. The rage from her not only tricking me but not showing any remorse, not a single sign of guilt as she broke my heart and sold my soul. I am not going to let that bitch send me to this place.

I push Father Windtalker's hands off my shoulders. "Let's Go," I say as I charge forward into the darkness. Father Windtalker smirks and pushes the glowing orb ahead of us. My shadow leads the way into the eternal night.

The deeper we go, the more the airport's tunnels and structures become corridors of the living embodiment of Dante and David Cronenberg works fused together. Rotting but animated corpses line the walls with their entrails crisscrossing over our heads. The diverging corridors we pass contain different forms of eternal torture enacted against the souls sent here. Unimaginable screams bellow from the corridors, each one still begging for God to forgive and release them from this eternal torment.

One corridor I peer into has a cuttlefish the size of a car with a head of a spider dismembering the living bodies of people who are screaming in agony and then throwing the parts against the walls, painting the walls with the splatter. The creature toys with a woman in a business suit by letting her crawl away as she tries to escape to our corridor. I am about to run to help her, but Father Windtalker grabs my shoulder and tells me to watch. It's toying with her and she has a minor moment of hope and almost makes it out, until the creatures' razor-sharp tentacle wrap around her legs and rip them from her torso. She screams in excruciating pain and terror as she looks behind and sees the creature devour her legs with its mandibles. In desperation, she crawls with blood gushing out of her mangled stumps, but the creature picks her up and throws her like a ragdoll against the wall, and makes her watch as it slowly carves her body into pieces and eats each one.

Before I can chastise Father Windtalker for not letting me save her, he sternly looks me in the eye and says, "I don't want your misplaced heroism to make our presence known to the demons and monsters. That woman deserves to be here. They all do. Their fate has been dealt. They chose to live their lives as selfish and immoral people. They were given plenty of times in life to save themselves, but they couldn't even face their demons; now they are forever tormented by them, and it's not your reasonability to try and save them."

"How do you know that?" I argue. "How do you know they weren't misjudged like me?"

"You're going to Hell because you're a fucking dumbass who let his dick cloud your judgment against an obviously bad decision with a woman who had evil and crazy written on her forehead," Father Windtalker snarks back.

I punch him in the jaw, causing him to fall back against the wall where a swarm of dismembered arms wrap around him and try to rip him apart. I run over and tear him away from their grasp.

Both of us breathing heavily, we stare uncomfortably at each other before he breaks the silence.

"I, along with everyone who knows what happened to you, don't believe you should be going here and God is wrong for not forgiving you. Yeah, you were a fucking dumbass for letting that tramp trick you, but you're a good man who doesn't deserve this. You, like many others in life, let love blind you, and you made a mistake of not stepping back and seeing the real picture. Unlike the rest of these fucks, you didn't commit any selfish or evil acts; you did the wrong thing for the right reasons, and I don't want to see a good man be sent here. Plus, I don't want to get stuck here because you have a hard-on for a woman in distress."

Father Windtalker's levity lightens the tense moment as my shadow makes a sudden shift to the tunnel ahead. We quickly follow it deeper into the void as the darkness begins to fade and a sickly pale light overcasts it. Even though the darkness is unnerving, the light is unimaginably disturbing as it now illuminates an unforgiving and terrible landscape in front of us as we exit the tunnel. It is a land of utter hopelessness and cruelty.

Inversed pyramids float in the air with horrific creatures crawling over their surfaces. Monoliths made of corpses pierce the sky. Temples resembling many holy sites on Earth are now desecrated effigies with bat-like creatures the size of men nesting on them.

In the distance, I see behemoths with demons chasing after people for sport, hunting them down and massacring them across the land. The awe-inspiring giants patrol the destitute land, while in its center is an abyss which no light can penetrate. My shadow guides us to the edge of the abyss and then settles underneath my feet.

I look into the abyss and feel overwhelming terror and madness. There are unbelievable roars of beast's unseen with the screams of help coming from the void within the abyss. Though I cannot see the bottom of it, I feel something sinister looking back at me. I look over at Father Windtalker and for the first time see terror on his face as he peers into the abyss.

"Father, what do we do now?"

He takes a moment to compose himself and begins chanting in tongues as he writes symbols and Latin scriptures into the black sand underneath our feet. As he performs his spell, I look to my left and see a field of crosses close to us. I walk over and can hear the mournful apologies to God followed by the prayers of the Catholics. On the crosses are men wearing various religious garbs rotting against their bloodied flesh.

As I walk closer, I realize these are Christian priests being tortured, each in a horrid creative way. One is made to swallow a red-hot crosier that seared his flesh as it made its way down his throat. The others are made to kneel on a bed of nails as the weight of the cross on their shoulders gets heavier and heavier and the nails penetrate their knees. Their spines snap underneath the cross, and their mangled bodies are also impaled by the nails. Some are forced to build walls made with scorching-hot jagged boulders which lacerate and sear their skin. They build the walls with each boulder causing excruciating injuries to their bodies, and randomly the walls collapse on the tortured priests, snapping their bodies like twigs.

But one Priest catches my attention. I walk closer to him as he is nailed to the cross with his front of the body against the beams but his neck savagely twisted, his head now facing his back. A sharp spear protrudes from the ground and plunges into his anus while a large nail is slowly inserted into his penis. He screams in agony and begs for it to stop, but the torture increases with each plea. When he drops his head, he stops crying and sees me.

"Hello, Father Glass."

The priest on the cross is Father O'Malley, the man whose confession sent me down this path; at least pedophiles get special treatment in Hell. He screams again and then composes himself to talk to me in garbles.

"He knows..." Father O'Malley says as he coughs up blood and pieces of organs. "He knows what you are trying to do."

A deathly cold shiver strikes through me. "How does he know and how come we haven't been attacked?"

Father O'Malley screams again in pain as the nail is inserted deeper into his shaft. "You have meddled with things no human should ever be involved with, your interactions with gods and monsters have been heard throughout the different realms of existence."

He chokes up blood again and continues, "You have done brave things that no man should do, and Lucifer has taken noticed. You have become a folk hero to the lost souls in Hell with the idea of hope spreading among us, that we could escape because of you."

"Escape because of me?"

"You don't walk into the House of the Devil without him knowing. You didn't infiltrate hell; hell opened its doors for you. That's why none of these unimaginable monsters have attacked you and your guide."

"Why? What would be the purpose?"

"The back door you are creating, do you think you would be the only one who would escape out of it?"

I stand in silence and shock at the idea that we are being led into a trap.

"The Devil loves to mock God, and he is reveling in the idea of a good man going to Hell. We all know, we all have heard the stories, and that's why we are have hope for you, but the Devil wants to make you into an example by spitting in God's face again. If you create that backdoor, then he will let the demons, monsters, and the unimaginable escape through it while you watch over it for eternity. You are to stand an inch from sweet escape but never know it as you will watch the horrors of Hell inflicted on the innocent because of your choice. You will feel every pain, every tear, and every loss from the people hurt from your escape plan. The Devil let you in to taunt you." He begins to cry in agony as the spear and the nail are inserted deeper into his orifices.

I try to find a rational reason why he might lie to me or trick me into not following through with my plan, but he is right. It was far too easy to walk through Hell undetected; even when we were exposed, we still haven't been attacked.

"Why would you tell me this?" I ask reluctantly. "Why would you help me?"

He manages to hold back his screams and confess to me, "I deserve to be here for molesting those boys and forsaking my vows. I deserve the eternity of torture, but I will not allow an innocent person back on Earth to be inflicted by the horrors of this God-forsaken place. I'm sorry for what has happened to you, but you and I must do whatever we can to protect the innocent. I failed in this regard when I was alive, but I have to try now because no innocent person should ever know what true Hell is."

Without another word I run back to Father Windtalker and yell out to him, "Stop the spell, it's a trap!" I stop in front of him, panting and sweating, and tell him what Father O'Malley said.

He looks angered that I gave away our position but he isn't an idiot, and he realizes that it was indeed too easy for us to make our way through Hell.

"Are you sure?" Father Windtalker asks as he continues writing the incantation on the ground. "This is your last means of escape; you will be stuck in Hell."

The ground begins to shake violently with the screams and roars of unimaginable creatures within the void. I begin to cry as I realize that going to Hell is unavoidable, that my choice will forever condemn me to Perdition. I look over to Father Windtalker who has a tear rolling down his cheek and know he doesn't need to hear an answer. He wipes the incantation from the ground with his foot, grabs me by the arm and we start running back the way we came, but our exit is blocked by the cuttlefish-spider monster we saw earlier. Demons, Behemoths, and other horrifying beasts begin to swarm around us, surrounding us. The trembles and the loud roars from the void behind us become louder as the unimaginable horror is climbing to the surface.

"I need a minute!" Father Windtalker screams as he falls to his knees and begins to chant.

I can't believe the horrifying creatures from all myths coming for us; Cthulhu is approaching from the horizon. A horde of demons soaked in the blood and organs of the tortured are advancing fast and about to be upon us. I look back at Father Windtalker chanting and know that we both might not escape, but he doesn't deserve to be here.

I run toward the horde in a futile attempt to fight them off. I am going to lose, but it will give enough time for Father Windtalker to escape. I run ten yards and am stopped by a figure which emerges in front of me. Father O'Malley stands between us and the hordes. His pelvis is ripped apart with his organs spewing out of his orifices, his hands are mangled, but his head is snapped back into position.

He screams, "Go! You don't deserve to be here!" He runs to the hordes and fights them off. He is being torn apart, but he has bought us time.

Father Windtalker stops his chanting and a bright light manifests in front of us. From the light stands the massive blue Mustang with fire coming from its eyes and its hooves scorching the ground of Hell.

The creatures of Hell bellow a horrific scream and continue to come after us. Father Windtalker grabs me and forces me on to the back of the Mustang. I reach over and take his hand to lift him up, but a demon snatches his leg and tries to take him away. The Mustang starts to kick and wail against the hordes as I use all of my strength to keep the Father with me. He looks at me in terror as the Demon's claws tear through his leg and lock on.

I feel his grip loosen and I panic as I can't hold on to him, I might lose him in Hell. His fingers almost slip through my grip and he is about to be taken by the horde until Father O'Malley emerges. Mangled, missing flesh and an arm; he swings an ax at Father Windtalker's leg and severs it. Father Windtalker screams in agony, but I pull him up on the Mustang with me. The Mustang gives out a majestic wail, and a brilliant light surrounds us followed by a wild gallop into it.

I awoke and saw the Mustang was a statue again but with plumes of smoke and steam coming off it, and claw marks on its hide. The first rays of dawn began to emerge, and I can see the landing planes and the Denver Airport again. I rolled over to my side and began to vomit and saw Father Windtalker doing the same until he screamed in agony.

I ran to him as he was grasping for his leg but what remained was only a mangled stump gushing with blood.

I rushed him to the hospital and after a day of surgery he was stabilized. The police had come to investigate but immediately left after they realized it was Father Windtalker, he indeed has a strong influence over the police. I sat with him for hours after the surgery, waiting for him to wake up. When he finally awoke he looked over at me, gave me a smirk and demanded his joints.

"You can't smoke in the hospital," I reminded him.

"The fuck I can't, I need a joint after this bullshit."

I went through his coat and found one. He took a deep hit and let it mellow in his lungs before exhaling it. He looked down at his stump and massaged it with his hand.

"I am sorry that I got you involved," I said. "You didn't deserve this. Nobody does but me."

Father Windtalker took another deep hit and said, "Don't start this self-pity shit with me. You didn't, and no one can never force me to do anything I don't want to do. I knew the risks of our mission; it was my fault for not seeing the trap. I'm thankful you weren't the pussy I thought you were and you hung on to me."

He squirmed in pain as he shifted himself to look at me. He looked sorrowful as he said, "I'm sorry I failed you. Losing my leg is nothing compared to the guilt I feel for not helping your fucking dumb ass save your soul. But, if it means something; you showed honor in Hell. I saw that you were about to sacrifice yourself to save my ass back there. God is a cunt for not seeing past your mistake."

I reached over, and he handed me the joint and I took a deep hit of it. "He may be a cunt, but he is the gatekeeper...and I think this is it. This is the end of the line for me. I am going to Hell, and there is nothing I can do now. No one else to help me, no weapon, no gods, no spells. Nothing. I have to accept my fucking destiny."

I suddenly stood up, flinging my chair behind me, and with all of my strength punched a hole in through the wall. "I am going to Hell because I loved the wrong woman. I am going to Hell because I couldn't see past the façade, the con. I am going to Hell because I made the decision. The one thing that God asks of us is to protect our souls, the gift of existence. To nurture it and make something beautiful of it, and I sold it like it was some cheap knickknack at a garage sale. I can blame that bitch Lilith all I want for conning me, but the decision was always mine, the responsibility was always mine."

The nurse came in and was about to call security on me, but it turned out Father Windtalker also had influence over the hospital when he mentioned who he was and showed her a picture from his phone of a few executives of the hospital and him golfing. After she left, he looked at me and told me to take another deep hit.

"Llewyn, there are things beyond our comprehension and our power. There are Gods, Devils; monsters, physics, science; politicians...whatever else that is more powerful than the individual. But it's the individual, the person who realizes that despite the odds against them, they too have the power to create miracles. No matter what religion or myths you research, there are always stories of an individual willing to go against the gods because they have a power the gods can never have, the power to create their own fate. You still have time, Llewyn. Every second you still have on this planet is a chance to change your fate. This isn't the time to give in to failure and the overwhelming odds against you, this is the time when a man can become a miracle."

The room went silent, and I took a final hit. "Where do I go from here?" I asked.

Father Windtalker motioned for the joint, and he took a hit after I gave it to him. He took a drag and smiled, "Well, there is a house in New Orleans…"

House of the Rising Sun

New Orleans, Louisiana. September 9th, 2015

The taxi drove past a strangely quiet Bourbon Street and headed south away from the lights of the skyscrapers and into the bayou. I told Sister Abigail of the house I was visiting on the suggestion from Father Windtalker and surprisingly she had no information; not for lack of trying but New Orleans is a strange and secretive world on its own.

I hadn't seen any houses for a few minutes until we stopped at the edge of a deserted, narrow driveway. I stepped out of the cab and into the humid bayou air with the worn cobblestone road underneath my feet. The driver quickly sped away without me paying because he knew, as did all the locals, of the house at the end of the street. I slowly walked down the long and dark cobblestone driveway. There was one dull lamp on the street, but its rays of light were snuffed out by the massive Live Oak trees that wrapped around the property. Even though it was humid, and my sweat ran down my back like a water rapid, there was a cold chill running down my body as I saw the dull lights of the old plantation house at the end of the driveway.

The house's once white paint was now a sickly yellow with patches of dried paint peeling off slowly with the passing of each sun. I walked onto the old creaking porch and felt somebody watching me from behind. I turned around and shrieked as I saw a dozen pairs of red eyes staring back at me from the other end of the driveway. I knocked feverishly against the large door as I felt the red eyes approach the house. There was no answer, only the snap of branches behind me and a subtle groaning. I panicked and began banging on the door as hard as I could, but still no answer. Then, I heard a footstep onto the porch, and the hairs on my neck stood up; I was too terrified to turn to see the creatures. I banged harder until the door suddenly swung open, and a hand reached out and pulled me inside, with the door slamming shut behind me.

I was brought inside a waiting room with velvet-trimmed walls, a coat rack, and a small leather couch. The massive hand, which was still holding onto me, was attached to a massive black man who was two feet taller than me, wearing a waistcoat with no shirt and a bowler hat. Tattoos of alligators, saints, and snakes cover his chest and arms, and a necklace of bones hung from his thick neck. He stared me down intensely for a few moments as my nerves were still trembling from the creatures outside.

"I'm here to see someone about..." I began to say.

The hulking doorman interrupted with his thick Cajun accent, "I know why you here, maan. Père Windtalker called, and said yo brown ass would be coming."

The black hulk opened the waiting room door where I was greeted by the sounds of a lively party. He led me into the main house, and I was amazed by the eclectic decorations: statues of Catholic saints, oil paintings depicting life on the plantations over 200 years ago; skulls of alligators, bulls, and men hung from the walls. A large iron cross hung above the stairs right next to a painting of a beautiful black woman wearing bright Creole garb and holding a giant yellow python. I was led into the main parlor where the focal point of the strange, diverse party was. Wealthy white socialites were sharing drinks and stories with gang leaders from the Ninth Ward. There were black professors wearing LSU pins on their lapels, playing poker with the overall-wearing, white fishermen.

"This is neutral ground, Brown Sugar," said a sultry voice coming from behind me. I turned around and marveled at the woman's unearthly beauty.

She had smooth dark skin with long flowing black hair with streaks of red in it. She wore a tight burgundy gown that accented her small waist, curvy hips, and bountiful breasts, with a yellow leather boa wrapped around her neck and arms. I was infatuated with her until I was caught off guard by the hissing sound coming from her. The leather boa around her neck was a live snake.

She began to laugh as she brought the snake's head to her face and gave it a little kiss. "Don't let old Zombi scare you. He doesn't even like live rats." She giggled as she handed the boa to the doorman. "Merci, Legba. I'll take Monsieur Glass from here." She wrapped her arm around my arm and guided me through the lavished house.

"For generations, this house has served as a place for all of New Orleans' affluent and powerful people to come and meet."

She led me through the crowded den where I saw a high-ranking police officer shooting pool with a baggy clothed man with Air Jordan's on his feet and prison tattoos on his arms and neck.

"There aren't any fights here?" I asked. "You have people from different parts of society, criminals shooting pool with cops, and blue-collar men drinking with corporate raiders, how come there is no animosity?"

"They were all raised in New Orleans, and they know of the legend of this house, so they fear the stories of what might happen to them if they violate my rules. I have taught them to fear me."

"And who are you?" I asked

"To you? A friend of a friend but call me Mademoiselle."

She led me to the staircase and guided me up the stairs where I got a closer look at the old paintings and I noticed how much the woman on my arm looked like the women in the vintage pictures.

She led me upstairs past closed bedroom doors, where I heard the gentle moans and laughs of sinful delights taking place. We walked to the end of the hallway, and up another dark staircase which led into the attic. Mademoiselle opened the door, and I was struck with awe with the amount of history I saw hanging on the walls. Paintings of New Orleans both old and modern, old farming tools rusted from age and use in the fields. A massive shelf on the wall held bottles of herbs and other medicines in glass mason jars, religious relics from Catholicism and totems from Africa, but what caught my eye was the pictures. There was a smaller version of the painting of the woman above the staircase hanging behind a large old oak desk at the end of the attic.

Elegantly framed photographs were all over the attic. All the pictures were of the plantation house and the staff that worked in it throughout the decades since the house was opened. The oldest dated photo was from 1830, and the last one was taken in 2015. I marveled at the history captured in the old black and white photographs, but something stood out to me. Something I could not place. They all shared something in common besides the house in the picture. Before I could put two and two together, Mademoiselle called for me.

"Come stand in the light for me, Llewyn," she said softly to me in her sultry voice.

I stood in the light, and she stared at my shadow for a few moments in silence with a curious look on her face. I couldn't help but stare at her, she was overwhelmingly beautiful and the burgundy dress made her even more enticing. Without looking up, she asked, "Do you think you did the right thing?"

I was taken aback by the bluntness of the question. "I don't know...I thought I did."

"Do you think your intentions were pure?"

"Why does it matter? I doomed either way."

Without looking up, she walked over to the shelf of medicines and herbs and started pulling jars down. "Do you think you're a good man?" she asked as she began to mix herbs into a marble grinder.

"I thought I was."

She stopped grinding the herbs, turned around and slowly and seductively walked toward me. She smiled and said, "We are about to find out."

She quickly lifted her hand and blew a thick black powder in my face. I pushed myself away from her and started coughing violently as my lungs burned and my eyes watered. I collapsed to the floor and tried to crawl away but I lost control of my body. I began to panic and felt dread take over as Mademoiselle knelt next to me and gently caressed my face with her hand as I passed out.

I found myself in a dream where I was floating in a black abyss. I could not move, but I felt my body shake violently when I heard the familiar voice call for me from the abyss. "You, like all men, want to be the hero," Lilith said arrogantly. "You were the only one stupid enough to believe in love."

I cringed at hearing that voice which was followed by heavy, moist breathing from behind me. Beyond the void was a massive silhouette of the Devil with an inferno's hellish glow behind it which only highlighted the size of him; his eyes reflected a blood-red gleam through the flames.

"Your time is coming, Mister Glass. Your debt will be paid. No matter how many places you travel to, no matter how many people you ask for help, you will end up here with me."

I couldn't move or scream but only cry as I felt doom come over me as I realized the futility of my efforts. I am going to hell, and it's my fault. I made the wrong choice for the wrong woman. I closed my eyes and opened them again, but this time I found myself standing back in the attic.

I was erect, but I couldn't move. I was incoherent and couldn't speak a word, but I was aware of my surroundings. The attic was now lit by a mass of red candles, and the desk had been cleared and made into an altar with men's skulls, candles, and a dead chicken. I could smell the strong bitter odor of incense lingering in the air when something sensational also caught my nose.

Legba walked into my peripheral vision and wheeled a cart with trays of the muffuletta, boiled craw daddies, and jambalaya gumbo. The smell and sight of the delicious food overwhelmed me as I stood helplessly locked in my body. Legba reached his massive hand behind my neck and pulled something out of my skin. Immediately my body jolted toward the cart. I couldn't help but devour the succulent entries laid before me. I was not even hungry, but I desired it, and I could not control my urges.

As I was about to break open a crawdaddy, I felt a prick behind my neck and my muscles locked in position; I was paralyzed again. Legba took the crawdaddy from my grip and wiped my mouth with a silk handkerchief. He wheeled the cart away and left the attic.

I then felt somebody pull me from behind and straighten me like I was a poseable mannequin. I smelled her infectious perfume first as she slowly, teasingly moved in front of me. Mademoiselle looked more provocative than ever as she was now wearing a short red skirt which shown her full thick thighs, and a red and black shawl which showed her flat stomach.

She stood face to face with me and stared at me with her large, lovely brown eyes. She wrapped her arms around my neck, and I felt something come out of my neck again. I could not control myself as I picked her up and made her legs straddle my hips. I kissed her deeply and passionately as I carried her to the altar. She moaned slightly as I reached up her skirt and she grabbed my neck. I felt the pinch again, and I was stuck straddling her on the altar. She smiled and kissed me on my lips before she climbed out from underneath me. She grabbed a jar from next to the altar and blew more dust into my face and I went into another deep sleep.

I awoke again standing erect, but this time I was behind the altar, and shirtless men were wearing lifelike masks of bull's heads chanting in what sounded like a mix of Haitian, Latin, and French. Mademoiselle walked between the men holding a decapitated chicken spraying the leaking blood onto the men. The chanting became louder and faster as she began to dance provocatively. I wanted to run and escape, but my muscles were locked and no longer in my control.

As she danced faster and more erratically the men made a passage for Legba as he walked in wearing white face paint and carrying an unconscious woman in a white gown. Mademoiselle danced around Legba and smeared blood on the chest of the woman as he lay her down on the altar.

The chanting became louder and faster. Mademoiselle danced around the altar toward me and started to smear blood on my chest. Legba came to my other side with a sharp dagger and opened my hand. My heart raced fearing he might cut off a finger, but he placed the handle in my palm and closed my grip. The chanting came to an immediate halt, and Mademoiselle stopped dancing and stood across the alter from me.

"You traveled a great distance to break this curse, and you came to me to see if I was your salvation. A pardon for the condemned man I see in front of me. I have a way to set you free, but your salvation is in your hands. Take the dagger and plunge it into this woman's heart and she will take your place in Hell."

I was disgusted but not for the act of killing her, but that I contemplated doing it. To be set free from going to Hell would only cost the life of a stranger. I considered it for what felt like hours but just moments passed. Legba reached behind my neck and I felt another pinch. Suddenly my arm shot up above me as I held the dagger above my head ready to plunge it into her heart. But my arms stood stiffly above me and I felt the dagger shaking in my hand.

"No," I murmured.

"Do it!" Mademoiselle yelled as she leaned over the table pointing her fingers furiously at my face. "You take that knife and sacrifice her."

My hands shook violently as I still held the dagger over my head. "No," I said louder this time.

"She doesn't deserve to live. She stole from her family, cheated on a man that loved her, and she killed a child with her car when she was high on a heroin binge. She drove off and left the child to die. If she had stopped and helped he might have lived, but she fled like the coward she is. Take the knife and plunge it into her yella heart! Let a truly guilty person go instead of an innocent man."

Temptation flooded me. If I did it, then I got a second chance, and if it's true what Mademoiselle said, then I'll be serving justice. If it's a lie, then I would have killed an innocent person, and it wouldn't matter because I was still going to Hell.

I stood over the unconscious woman and watched her chest rise and fall with each shallow breath. She moved her head slightly, and I saw a glint of light reflecting from a tear rolling down her cheek.

My arms fell forward as I threw the dagger behind me. I fell against the altar and began to sob. "I can't do it... I can't do it."

A smile spread across Mademoiselle's face as she slowly began to clap. Legba came to my side and brought a cup of ripe smelling tonic to my mouth.

"Drink," he said softly.

I gulped down the bitter drink as Legba guided me to an old leather chair and sat me down in it. I slowly felt control over my body come back as I sat back and watched the men in the bull masks slowly exit the room. To my surprise, the unconscious woman rose from the table and hugged Mademoiselle. Mademoiselle reached into her bra and pulled a few hundred-dollar bills from her cleavage and gave it to the woman.

"Merci, belle" Mademoiselle said as she kissed her on each cheek.

"What the hell is going on? What did you do to me?" I yelled while trying not to fall out of the chair.

The woman left the attic with Legba right behind her. Mademoiselle sat down on top of the altar and leaned forward toward me, close enough for me to get a whiff of the intoxicating perfume again.

She reached into her cleavage again but brought out a thin brown cigarillo and lit it with a candle that was on the altar.

"Brown Sugar," she affectionately said to me. "What happened here on this wonderful evening was proof for me that you may have a chance of getting your soul back."

"What do you mean?"

"This whole show we put on for you was a test."

"This...this was all an act? What was that dust you blew into my face? What happened to me with the food and you? What was that thing on my neck? You were going to have me kill another person for a sick fucking test?" I was fuming in between breaths, but Mademoiselle kept her composure and smiled.

"That dust was a mixture of nightingale, marijuana and other herbs and roots I collected over the years. It stops a person from having inhibitions when inhaled; it stops your self-control. Legba and I had to test it to see if it works on you, so we first put my irresistible home cooking in front of you to see if you could control yourself, and you couldn't."

"If it worked then what was the whole seduction test for?"

She smirked, "Double checking if it works. Plus, you're a cutie."

"How did you know I was attracted to you? You might not have been my type."

"Please," as she motioned with her hands and confidently showed off her physique.

"But you were going to have me kill someone, how did you know I wouldn't do it?"

Mademoiselle slid off the altar, walked behind me, then came back around and sat back down in front of me with the dagger. She took the blade and pressed into the palm of her other hand.

She smiled and plunged it into herself. I jumped up to stop her, but I did not see the blade exit through the other side of her hand. She started to laugh and plunged the knife into her leg. That's when I saw the blade retracting into the hilt.

"I got this at a magic store, Brown Sugar. It's a prop knife. Plus, Legba was behind you the whole time. He would have broken your arms if you did try to do it. The woman is a bartender who works downstairs; she loves being a part of my acts."

"What about the thing behind my neck, how come I couldn't move?"

Mademoiselle reached down her cleavage again and pulled out a tiny pin.

"Acupuncture pin. There is a nerve in the back of your neck we placed a pin in. It paralyzes you while its in."

I stood straight out of my seat and began to yell. "So this was a fucking act? Can you even save my soul, or did you waste the precious time I have left for your amusement?"

She smiled calmly, and it seemed to put me at ease. "No, I can't save your soul, but there is a chance you can save it yourself."

"What?"

"When people make deals with the Fallen One, they usually do it for power, money, or youth. You did it for another reason. You made a deal with the Devil to save a life, even if that life ended up betraying you. From all my years of practicing Voodoo and communing with demons and Loa's, I have heard a few stories of the possibility of someone escaping the Devil, but they all had required one thing in common."

"Which is?"

"A good heart. I needed to see tonight if I were to take away your self-control would your heart remain true, and indeed it has."

Distraught, I walked over to the wall of pictures and stared at them silently. Was there a chance of me escaping Hell? And what was so odd about these antique pictures?

"So, you can't help me?" I asked as I tried to figure out the pictures.

"No," she said from behind me. "You'll have to do this on your own."

That is when I noticed what the pictures all had in common, Mademoiselle was in each one.

She walked up next to me and smiled as she handed me a piece of paper. "Go and face your Demon..."

I opened up the paper, and it was her phone number.

"Give me a call if you survive, Brown Sugar."

I became flustered but I was curious about the pictures, and after this odyssey, I wouldn't be surprised if she was another goddess.

"Thanks, Mademoiselle. But what about these pictures, why are you in all of them?"

"Good genes," she said sarcastically. "And you can stop calling me Mademoiselle. The name is Marie Laveau."

The Reckoning

Fenway, Massachusetts

October 31st

03:20 am

"There are other stories," Llewyn said as he looked at his watch. "But it's time to pay the Devil his due."

I sat in awe, looking at Llewyn Glass after he finished his tales of mystery and horror. I was engrossed to the point that I had lost track of time and didn't notice that the storm had grown malevolently fierce. Even my patrons were captivated by his tale as they did not leave nor ask for more drinks. He sat back in his seat, took a final gulp and held the glass to his lips as he sadly savored his last sip. The patrons looked at us and then stared at me as they all wanted to me ask the question we all had come to wonder.

"Mister Glass, how can we know what you said is true? What proof do you have of this ludicrous story?"

Right then the blinding white glare of lightning filled the pub, and the earth-shattering rumble of thunder shook the bar as we stared in silence at the shadowy Llewyn Glass.

He slid out of the booth and walked to the middle of the pub and asked the Sheriff to shine his light on him. The Sheriff, with his hand reluctantly quivering, un-holstered his light from his belt and shined it upon Llewyn. In an instant, we all simultaneously gasped at the incredible and uncanny sight; his shadow was cast in front of him. The Sheriff walked around Llewyn in disbelief as no matter where his light shined the shadow always cast in front of Llewyn.

"It's all true, all of it," the Sheriff said terrified.

"If all of it's true, then that means..." before I could finish my sentence, the storm suddenly fell dead, and an unnerving silence filled the air. The lights in the pub began to dim as a ghastly red glow which came from the graveyard took its place. The town nurse looked out the window and became ghostly white as she walked back nervously and tripped over a chair.

All of us pushed and made room on top of each other to peer out the windows as we stared into the graveyard and looked upon the horror that was finally here.

At the edge of the cemetery, next to the tree line of the woods, was a large and imposing silhouette standing on the mound of a fresh grave with another smaller silhouette shoveling dirt out of the grave.

We couldn't see clearly what the silhouette looked like, but we felt it staring back at us, sending chills and doom through our bodies. I turned around and found Llewyn at the broken jukebox. He ripped the out-of-order sign off it and gently caressed the machine. The lights flickered in the box and then went dead again. Llewyn looked down in silence and pressed three buttons and stared at the jukebox for a few moments. It did not turn back on.

I stared at the man who had amazed me with wonder and horror from his story, but now I felt only sadness and pity as we listened to a man make his final confession before his death. He had done his best to hide his fear and grief when he engrossed us with his tale, but now a few tears fell from his chin, and his hands shook violently. But he held himself up with dignity and wiped his tears with his handkerchief.

Llewyn was afraid but not a coward. He was facing his Demon, our Demon, and he wasn't going to back down. He could have kept running, he could have used the Archangel's spear; he could have kept the backdoor to hell open; but Llewyn is an archetype, he is a hero. He is facing the embodiment of evil, and he will not run from it.

Llewyn Glass walked to the door but stopped to straighten himself, fixed his tie, and buttoned his suit coat. The patrons moved out of his way, afraid to be near him as the Devil might take them to hell too; but not I. I quickly ran behind him and yanked his hand. I spun him around and embraced him. I kissed him hard as he held me tight. I could feel him wanting to not let go, and I held him as if he still had a chance of escaping. I could feel his heart race with wanting to stay, to escape but because who he became, or who he had always been, he had to face oblivion himself and do it on his own terms.

"You're a good man, why do you have to do this?" I asked rhetorically in between kissing him and crying.

I kissed and cried for this man because he renewed my faith; not in God, but in man. That man, as a species, could become something much more then what we are. We can become holy even in the face of damnation by choosing to be good. By choosing to do the right thing even in the face of inevitable doom. That mankind has a chance to live up to its potential.

Llewyn gently let me go. The others no longer backed away from him but said their goodbyes with hugs and handshakes; a hero's farewell. The blinding lightning flashed again, and a crash of thunder violently shook the ground. Some of us fell and bottles of alcohol shattered as they dropped off the shelves. The Devil tolls for Llewyn Glass. He hugged me one last time and gave me a passionate kiss goodbye.

He slowly walked to the door but stopped and without looking back said, "To answer your question, Lorelai, I have to get own my soul back. To no longer accept the judgment of an unseen God who no longer sees me as a worthy man, but to rely on who I am and to know the truth for myself.

"If you learned anything tonight, then please remember these words: you should live a balanced life of responsibility and hedonism. Be kind and unapologetically honest, especially with yourself. Be compassionate but vicious when the situation calls for it. There are those who are shaped and molded, and those who define. Choose which one you want to be. Find a lover who says no for the right reasons. There are those who seek and those who understand. There are those who kill and those who spare. There are those who follow the road and those who make their own path. You can be whichever but be wise above all." Llewyn slightly cocked his head back and smirked at me.

The front door suddenly swung open as a vicious wind entered the Pub. He took one step forward into the dark night but stopped and looked me in the eye and said, "Remember, at the end of all things there is and shall always be hope."

The sound of scratching vinyl emanated from the jukebox as it came to life and the steady and heavy strokes of Johnny Cash's "The Man Comes Around" began to play. I watched as Llewyn strode courageously to the grave being prepared for him. He did not waver nor show any sign of fear but took a flask from his pocket and chugged what remained before tossing it among the tombstones.

He walked to the creature's silhouette in the darkest of nights, with only a blood moon lighting the graveyard. Never losing his footing, Llewyn kept his gaze on the creature as he walked arrogantly through the graveyard.

I stepped outside the bar with the Sheriff and a few others behind me. The Sheriff took a deep breath of air and began vomiting violently.

A few other patrons started to cough and choke from the rotting odor coming from the graveyard. I pulled a handkerchief from my pocket and covered my nose to snuff out the stench of putrefied flesh, sewage, and sulfur.

A swarm of cats who inhabit the graveyard ran through the patrons' feet and into the pub where they hid in any dark corner they could find. A flash of lightning struck behind the horrifying creature, and I caught a minuscule glance into the black void which surrounded it. I could not believe what I saw from the brief glimpse nor could I describe it, but my heart raced faster from the terror which took hold of it, and I succumbed to my nausea from the sight of the gruesome creature.

Despite all of this, Llewyn kept strutting confidently, never breaking stride, not even choking from the disgusting odor, but walked tall and faced his destiny. His final steps were slower, a taunting pace as he went to the foot of the mound and finally faced the Devil. Llewyn reached into his jacket pocket and took out a pack of cigarettes and his Zippo. His stance was bold and his face unwavering as he stood his ground in front of the Fallen One.

His only tell of complete fear was when his hand shook nervously as he placed the cigarette between his lips and lit it. He looked down as he took one long drag of his final cigarette alive and slowly stared into the creature's eyes.

The world went quiet at that moment. The strong wind, lightning, and the rustling tree branches stopped as Llewyn stood face to face with evil itself. We could hear each other's racing hearts in the eerie silence.

The creature overshadowed Llewyn with its towering size. It did not move but stared down into his soul as the dark figure next to the creature kept digging into the earth.

"Glad you came, Llewyn," the Devil said in a bloodcurdling gravely deep voice.

Its leathery robe shifted as it reached out its long-clawed hand. Llewyn took out another cigarette and gave it to the creature. The creature slowly brought the cigarette to its lips as the tip lit by itself. The creature's features were still cloaked by darkness but the dim light from the cigarette showed that the face was drenched in blood and its jaw had visible sinew with chunks of rotting flesh hanging off it.

"Your debt needs to be paid tonight," the creature gurgled. "You traded your soul for another, was she worth it?"

Llewyn took another drag of his cigarette and looked down in regret but didn't answer.

"I bet you wished she did die, that she was taking your place in Hell."

Llewyn stood silently against the creature's taunting.

The creature slowly pointed one of its claws to the figure digging the fresh grave.

"That would be for me?" Llewyn asked.

"Maybe...depends..." the creature's shrill answer cut through my ears.

"Depends on what...?"

The creature took the cigarette from its lips and brought it to the figure next to him. The cigarette burned brighter as it showed the creature's clawed and rotting fleshed limb as it pointed to the moving figure. I watched as Llewyn gasped in horror and took a step back.

"I thought it would be fitting to have Lilith dig your grave," The Devil said with glee.

"Llewyn, please help me," begged the haggard but handsome woman, caked with dirt dug from the grave, her raw hands smearing blood across her scorched dress.

"Quiet!" The Devil yelled in a voice which caused me to wet myself. "You don't get to con your way out of this one."

The horrifying creature backhanded her; her head snapped back violently with her jaw nearly torn off her face. I marveled in horror as the flesh of her severed jaw began to grow again with visible strands of muscle and flesh reattaching itself back to her face.

"What is she doing here!" Llewyn yelled over the rushing wind.

The creature brought the cigarette back to his mouth and took a long drag. "You impressed me. Out of all the souls I've collected and tortured over the past eons, you have to be the one I truly admire. Rebellious, cunning, and self-righteous; you remind me of a young me before I was cast out of Heaven. You also live by your own rules and never veer away from them... just like me. So, before your deal expires, I have a new offer for you: become my advocate on Earth and Lilith will take your place in Hell."

Caught off guard by the Devil's offer, Llewyn coughed violently as smoke and phlegm spewed out of his mouth.

"Yes, you wouldn't go to Hell, but neither would you enter Heaven because you are unforgivable to the pompous dick we call Father. Like Tithonus and Cane, you would live an eternity on Earth and never die, at least until I kick-start the Apocalypse; then we'll see if the predictions from the illiterate apostle were true. You will work for me and do my bidding on Earth, which won't be so bad because it will be fun to live in sin."

The Devil took a long drag and continued, "To sweeten the pot, I will make you rich, and I will get you anything you desire. I will make for you a Heaven on Earth as long as you work for me."

The wind blew harder as a torrential rain begun to pour from the black sky, soaking Llewyn and Lilith but leaving the Creature alone, as if the dark void surrounding him shielded him from the water. Llewyn stood there with the cigarette hanging to his side of his lips, no longer lit but soaked and limp. I could only see the side of his face from where I stood, but I knew from his look that he was considering on settling on an offer no mortal in his position would pass up. I wouldn't blame him if he did.

"Llewyn..." Lilith said as her jaw finished mending itself. "...please don't do this. I'm so sorry to have brought you into this, but you can't trust him. But you can still trust me, I still love you."

Llewyn for one brief moment looked her as only a lover could but the brief moment quickly ended as he flew into a rage. "Stop lying! You have the King of Lies standing next to you, but you still can't stop lying! Why shouldn't I take the deal? You conned me in selling my soul for your immortality! I wanted to spend my entire life with you. To wake up to you every morning...to have children together..."

Llewyn stopped for a moment to gasp for air from the overwhelming experience and wipe the rain from his red eyes. "The worst part wasn't the ordeal, it wasn't living with the heavy hopelessness of going to Hell, or finding out our relationship was a lie, or how evil a person you are; but I still think of you every day, and part of me hopes you'll come back. How is that for a curse? Not going to Hell but still being in love with the person who sent you there."

Lilith climbed out of the grave and crawled to Llewyn; wrapping her arms around his legs as she begged on her knees and cried for him not to do it

"I can't even tell if those tears are even real or if you are sticking to your act even at the gates of Hell. Tell me, why shouldn't I take the deal? Why shouldn't I let you go to Hell?"

Lilith sobbed louder but could not answer the question. For the first time in her life, I think she found out she couldn't get her way out of this. She was about to suffer the rage of a good man.

"That's right. Why shouldn't he take the deal?" The Devil taunted as he grabbed her leg and crushed it with one swift grasp as he threw her back into the grave; her head slammed against a tombstone and she was knocked unconscious.

The wind and rain grew more vicious as bolts of lightning struck behind the Pub. The earth rumbled, some patrons ran and hid while others couldn't move because they were too consumed by fear to do anything but watch. But, through the biblical chaos, Llewyn did not flinch. The storm-ravaged him, a cruel lover showed her face before his final breath, and he was facing the Devil; but Llewyn stood there staring eye to eye with the horrifying and grotesque embodiment of evil and refused to cower.

The creature flicked his cigarette onto Lilith's head as he lay in the grave and said solemnly, "The moment is here. Take the deal, Llewyn. You are the only one of God's wretched puss-filled mistakes that I respect. Most others would have wallowed in self-pity or delved into nihilism and hedonistic pleasures, but not you. I have respect for you, but neither of us will ever see Heaven. So please, take the deal."

Llewyn stood quietly for a few moments but then looked back and stared into my eyes with a raindrop running down his face, or maybe a tear. I saw that he had made his impossible choice.

"No."

The Devil took a step back as Llewyn made his brave decision. "You stupid fuck, why not take it?" the Devil said with fury.

"All I have left in this last moment on Earth is who I am; who I choose to be. If I'm going to Hell, then I am going to Hell as a good man."

The Devil lunged forward, grabbed Llewyn by the neck and lifted him off of the ground. The leathery cloak which draped the Devil was not a cloak at all but his wings as they unfolded and spread out over the graves. The leathery wings were not bat-like, as portrayed in movies but rat-like with hair and diseased flesh. His body was large and strong, but his skin was scorched and filleted. Pieces of rotting flesh hung across his body with maggots and roaches crawling out of his orifices.

"You fucking fool! Is this what you want? To die with some false honor so you can end up looking like this? You should have taken the fucking deal! Now I'm going to rape your ass for centuries. I will torture you to exhaustion with rest nor peace ever coming. I will make you my rag doll and tear your limbs off every day as they will constantly grow back. You will become the toy I will give to my lowest demons to be used as a distraction from their existence in Hell. And, when I have finally broken your spirit, I will remind you of this night and the choice you made on it, then I will start the process all over again. You will no longer know the pleasures of pissing and shitting, or even know what it is to close your eyes and forget. You will know no salvation, you stupid prick!"

The ground shook violently, and the air became frigid. I dropped to the ground and felt my blouse freezing to the wet grass. A black sphere with cracks of white light flickering out of it appeared behind the Devil. Horrifying screams for help and asking forgiveness from God were all around me, mixed in with the roars of beasts no imagination could produce. It was the gateway into Hell.

"Are you ready, Mister Glass?" The Devil roared as he dragged Llewyn by his neck toward the gate. I wanted to run to Llewyn and help him, but there was nothing I could do but stare in terror and awe. The Devil stopped at the threshold of the gate, picked Llewyn up off the ground and held him facing the Pub and us. "Enjoy this last precious moment of humanity and life because you will never know this again."

A single tear rolled down Llewyn's cheek, but he remained steadfast and refused to face perdition as a coward. The Devil took one step into the gate, and within that moment, multiple lightning bolts struck the mound on which they stood, and unimaginable screams deafened my ears.

Then silence fell. The entire cemetery was covered with a thick fog, but the storm, the Devil and Llewyn Glass were no longer with us.

The Sheriff and I remained frozen from fear. We did not move until the first break of dawn began to show. The Sheriff pulled out his sidearm, I grabbed a shovel next to a grave, and we cautiously entered the cemetery and approached the mound. The sun's rays were slowly illuminating the graves through the fog, but we both stopped simultaneously when we saw movement coming from Llewyn Glass's grave. I called out for Llewyn but didn't hear a response from whatever was moving there. The figure crawled out of the grave, and I rose my shovel to strike at whatever demon was left. The fog dissipated, and the rays of the morning sun showed to my shocking surprise who stumbled out.

"Am I still alive?" Lilith asked dazed in her soiled and blood-soaked dress. "Did Llewyn take the deal?"

A rage overtook me, and I blindly swung my shovel, striking her on the wrist. I heard the snap of bone and her cry of agony, which was cut short by my pouncing on her and punching her in the face as soon as she hit the dirt. The Sheriff pulled me away from her as I screamed, "You killed him! You killed him, you lying cunt! He was a good man who sold his soul to save you, and you killed him, you evil bitch!"

I fell to my knees onto the scorched earth and began to sob uncontrollably as I lost all hope in humanity, faith, and God. How could a benevolent God let this happen to a good man? How could a being who preaches forgiveness be so intolerant to a man who made the wrong decision for the right reasons? How could he be good when he lets evil win? Why should we care anymore about faith and doing what's right when one lapse of judgment could bring us damnation?

Lilith came to her feet, groaning from her mangled hand and busted face but something was odd about her. The Sheriff also looked at her as if he saw something strange. As the fog lifted entirely and the sun's rays shined brighter, our shadows cast to the right of us while Lilith's cast not with the direction of the morning sun, but in front of her. I was confused, did Llewyn take the deal at the last minute?

Behind Lilith a new sight caused me to go from crying with hopelessness to laughing madly with joy. Something that renewed my faith in not only humanity but all life itself. Upon casting my eyes on the mound, I was renewed and knew my family curse was indeed a blessing. Upon his grave, upon the place where the Devil condemned a good man had grown a single rose. A white rose. A sign of God's mercy.

Epilogue

October 31st, 2016

3:15 am

A year has passed since Llewyn Glass came into my family's pub. Some have denied what happened, not out of doubt of what they witnessed but to block the hellish memories of that night. Others stayed quiet and wished to never speak of what they saw again. The rest embraced his story and not only told the truth of what happened but helped spread his legend. The Sheriff made an official report of the incident, took evidence and witness testimony but let Lilith go because there is no law regarding making deals with Lucifer to arrest her for. Plus, she had worse problems to worry about than going to jail.

The public had mixed reactions, especially with how fantastical the events were. Despite the Government dismissing it as some elaborate promotional prank for the Crossroads Pub, the patrons from that night were interviewed by serious men from the FBI and the dirt was dug up from the mound where the Devil and Llewyn stood face to face.

Rumor has it that some of the soil and fragments from the scorched tombstone came back with elements not recognized on the periodic table.

The white rose, however, I dug up the morning Llewyn was taken and kept it hidden until the Feds left. To everyone's surprise, it has never wilted but still flourishes its bright white petals. I keep it now behind the bar in a closed glass case for all to see and judge for themselves if the story is true. Most think it's a fake or a clever prop created by some Imagineer at Disney because they touch it and it feels real, but it never dies. I find it illuminating in the dark when I close the Pub at night.

As for my faith in humanity and the things beyond it, I have been given a new perspective, which is something I am still reckoning with to this day. But, nonetheless, I am hopeful for the good in everyone, that we have as species have a chance at redemption. An individual is capable of heroic and legendary acts which require not the mightiest strike, the cruelest word, or the best lawyers, but a brave choice. Thanks to Llewyn Glass, I have spoken the truth about what happened in Afghanistan and have been able to bring closure to the families of my Marines.

The General who told me to lie and cover up the mission was questioned by the Senate and was stripped of his rank and dishonorably discharged. I still have to deal with the blow-back from going public with the truth, but it was worth it. My PTSD is gone, and I no longer want to kill myself but to embrace life, the good and bad parts of it. With great relief, I have chosen to adopt my family's business, both the Pub and the idea of being a witness to the strange and mythical.

Tonight, we had our annual pre-Halloween party before the tourists mob us tomorrow. The town of Fenway has sold out of hotels and Air B&B's, with the neighboring towns reporting the same. But, despite the great news of growth for our community and Pub, only a handful of the patrons from the year before showed up for our party. Thankfully, the Sheriff kept his job and embraced what happened to Llewyn Glass. The few who showed up talked about Llewyn and how he inadvertently changed their lives. One had beat his addiction to OxyContin and made amends with his family. One had become a whistleblower and informed the Feds of his accounting firm laundering money for drug dealers.

One patron was a petite and fragile woman who saved an oblivious boy by tackling him out of the path of a speeding car. We all traded stories with each other of how we have grown braver and more compassionate as people. While some had nightmares of what they saw, they still were grateful to share their issues with the other people who were there on the fateful night.

The patrons steadily left through the night until it was just me and the Sheriff. He insisted he would stay with me as I closed the Pub. He still hasn't asked me out, so I kissed him on the cheek and told him I was okay to close by myself, but he should take me out for breakfast in the morning. He left with the widest smile I have ever seen.

I was the last one left before the morning crew came in to ready the Pub for the massive party. I was walking to the trash out back when I saw something at the other end of the graveyard, at the tree line of the forest. My adrenaline kicked in, but I waited to see if it was some local kids or a tourist trying to "summon the Devil" with an Ouija board. I could only make out two figures as my eyes adjusted to the dark. One looked familiar, maybe someone from town, the other was a woman wearing what I could tell was a veil of a nun.

They hadn't noticed me, but both were crying and hugging each other. I could barely make out what was being said as I made my way closer, using the gravestones as cover. I stopped when I was close enough to make out what was being said, and I nearly shrieked when I recognized who the treacherous woman was. Lilith.

Lilith was in the arms of the nun, both crying hysterically.

"Mom, it's alright. Don't cry for me and don't blame yourself for what I have become. I have done terrible things just because I could. I have hurt many people and killed for no other reason than for my own twisted enjoyment. None of this is your fault. If the circumstances of my upbringing were different, I am sure I would have ended up the same. I am glad we spent time together before I go and pay my price for the life I chose to live. I am going to Hell because I deserve it, but I will no longer run from responsibility, but face it."

I felt a joy overcome me as Lilith was getting what she deserved, but I felt a small amount of sympathy for her because, in the end, she had chosen, like Llewyn, to face this Demon. Was she performing one last con in the hope of receiving God's forgiveness?

I don't know, and I am okay with not knowing because she walked into the forest by herself leaving Sister Abigail to grieve, but I quietly left with the notion that we all have a debt in the end. Some more than others, but some people are owed a second chance from God. But what I accept is that redemption knows no bounds and God might forgive her. That's his choice. But, Llewyn would have; such is the divinity of man.

The Rideshare: A Modern-Day Horror Story

"Bing," went the happy tone, notifying me of a new passenger to pick up. The sun was setting on a beautiful warm day, and for the first time in a while, I feel at peace with life. I have my first steady job in 2 years, and I've been doing Uber on the weekends to pay off my debt. The side-hustle is not bad; I wished it paid more since all the expenses are on the driver, but at least I get to meet some interesting people and some not so interesting folks like the two bachelors I just dropped off with one advising the other "You should offer to buy her Plan-B to show her you're sincere."

I made a U-turn on 3rd Street in my silver Ford Taurus and headed north to the passenger's location. This next passenger will be my last one; I want to get some dinner and enjoy my Friday night. It's been a while since I had some spending money and I was looking forward to bar hopping and checking out a live band. Maybe I'll get lucky tonight.

I was snapped out of my thoughts when a message from Jill, the passenger, pinged on my phone. She asked me to pick her up at Jack Russel park and wait for her in the parking lot. Usually, I'm hesitant about picking up a stranger in a park but it was in an affluent neighborhood, and there was a police station across from it; plus, she might be hot and single. I picked up a woman last year who invited me into her house for my tip. I've been hoping it would happen again ever since.

I pulled into the empty parking lot and swiped the icon on the app to notify her that I arrived. I looked around and saw nobody in sight other than the cars driving by on the street. My heart began to race. Something didn't feel right. I looked around one more time and saw no one in the park. No cars. No children on the swings. No joggers. Not even a policeman taking a smoke break outside the station. I went to cancel the ride and drive off but was startled when I heard the car's rear door open.

"Jill?" I asked.

The heavy metal click of the hammer of a gun being cocked rung in my ears and was followed by a hard cold muzzle pressed against the back of my head.

My eyes darted to the rear-view mirror and I saw the stainless-steel revolver jammed against my head. I followed the smooth-skinned but steadfast hand to a petite, curly brown-haired woman holding it. She hid her head behind the headrest before I could see her face. The barrel pressed harder against my head, her way of telling me to keep my eyes front.

"Listen, I don't have any money, and I'm not going to lose my life over a car. Just take what you want and leave me be. I haven't seen your face," I begged.

"Your phone. Take out the battery," she demanded.

I took a moment to steady my trembling hand before reaching for my phone, wishing there was an emergency button on the app to send a silent alert to the police. Wishing she'd sat in the front seat so I could overpower her small frame.

The phone and the battery were now apart, and I held them up to show them to her.

"Toss them."

I rolled down my window and threw them outside, the glass screen shattering on the asphalt. She then tapped something on my shoulder.

"The same thing with this one," Jill said.

I reached back and grabbed the object she was tapping on my shoulder. Confused, I hesitated when I saw her phone in my hands. The hesitation lasted for a brief moment as she nudged the gun in the back of my head again. Her phone came apart quickly and I tossed the pieces out too.

"Do you know where King's Lot is?" she asked.

"Poe and Flynn Street?"

"Yeah. Here are the rules and listen carefully because one deviation will lead you to a slow agonizing death as I shoot kneecap and kneecap then testicle and testicle in that order. Understand?"

"Yes," I spurted out. I was terrified and furious. I was scared to get my knees and balls blown out, but I also wanted to take the gun from her and beat her to death with it.

"Keep all the windows rolled up and take the backroads there. No sudden movements, no glances at me so you can make a plan and keep your hands on the wheel the entire time. Most of all, don't look back here, don't ever look at me— not one single glare. My gun is pointed at your spine the entire time I'm back here, remember that. Understand?"

"Yes."

"Drive," she ordered.

I drove out of the parking lot and made my way to the abandoned King's Lot car dealership. It was an infamous dealership known for its crooked deals and the federal prison time the owner and half the salesmen received for fraud. But it was the over-lavish 80's coke-fiend yuppie décor of the building that made it infamous. It reminded me of *The Wolf of Wall Street* meets *American Psycho* with its white walls and tiles, gold chandeliers and oil-paintings of historical battles. The place had become dilapidated by burglars and vandals and was now used as a smoking den for meth heads.

The drive there takes typically fifteen minutes but time was moving faster for me as my thoughts raced and my heart throbbed in panic. I heard movement coming from behind me, but I resisted the urge to look back. In the corner of my eye, I could only see her legs as she lay down on the back seat. I could dreadfully assume her gun was still pointed at my back.

I turned the corner on Flynn St. and was only a mile away from Poe. Sweat cascaded from my hands and off the steering wheel as I had five minutes before we arrived at our final destination. We stopped at a red light, and to my surprise, a police cruiser stopped in the turn lane next to us.

I wanted to jump out. I wanted to take the chance and run out of my car and get to the cop as fast as I could. I assumed Jill's silence meant she didn't see the police, maybe I had a chance. Maybe I wouldn't die.

But fear paralyzed me, stopping me from salvation, as I helplessly watched the cop make the left turn and go on with his shift, unaware of the strange kidnapping happening in the car next to him.

"I would have blown your balls off if you reached for the door handle," Jill said.

My teeth and asshole clenched as the Taurus pulled into King's Lot, coming to an unnerving stop. Ominous silence filled the air as I waited and prayed that I would be granted an escape of whatever horror she had planned for me.

The silence broke when she opened both back doors and did something with them for a moment. I quickly glanced into my side mirrors and saw her switching on the child safety locks on both doors.

"What the fuck..." I said baffled.

My door flew open, and my captor finally revealed herself. She was small, barely above five feet, and petite. She wore a white dress with a sunflower print matched with a pair of yellow Converses and a cornflower purse. Her brown curls paired beautifully with her green eyes and tanned skin; the only thing that was more distracting than her beauty was her revolver pointed to my head.

"Take this, now," she ordered as she handed me something palmed in her free hand. I held out my hand as she dropped a little blue pill into it. I looked down and saw the familiar "V" logo I'd seen on the erectile dysfunction commercials.

"What the fuck is going on?" I belted out. "Why did you kidnap me? Why are you forcing me to take Viagra?"

Her response was pressing the cold barrel against my head and counting down, "Five...four...three..."

I popped the bitter-tasting pill in my mouth and swallowed. Immediately she looked at her slim gold watch and noted the time.

"Get out slowly and turn your back toward me once you're out."

Following her orders, I left the safety of my car and Jill walked me into the abandoned building with her gun jammed in my back. Blood was no longer rushing to my legs but flowing to my engorging penis, which I desperately wished it wouldn't come erect. The mixture of the Viagra, adrenaline, terror, and utter confusion nearly caused me to heave out my lunch, but I held it in, afraid she might get trigger happy.

She walked me into a dark corner office, which stank of mold and piss, and had me lay flat on the soiled carpet, with my arms spread far apart. Jill kept her distance and had the advantage with me on the ground, which made tactical sense, but what she did next only added to the insanity. She reached underneath her dress and tore her panties off with a few hard yanks.

"I need you to listen carefully on what's going to happen next," she commanded. "I want you to unzip your jeans and pull them down to your knees. You're not to make eye contact with me and don't even fucking move your hands. If I see a finger lift off the ground, then I'm emptying the gun point-blank into your chest. Now tell me you understand."

"I do," I said as tears trickled down my cheek.

Jill stood over me for a moment, and I closed my eyes. She pressed the revolver to my chest, over my heart, and I felt her dry flesh around my pharmaceutically engorged member as she began to straddle me painfully. She pounded her hips against mine which made the pain excruciating as I felt the foreskin being torn off my penis and her vagina becoming lubricated from the blood. I wanted it to end. I wanted this fear and the rape to be a bad dream, hoping I was passed out at home and I was going to wake up from this terrible dream. But the terror and helplessness turned to a numb void as I went into shock with the last words mumbled out of my mouth, "Why are you doing this?"

Lucidity struck me hard as I felt something sharp dig into my forehead. I opened my eyes, and Jill's palm was over my face with her fingers digging into my scalp.

"What..." I said before she clawed her sharp nails across my face. I screamed in agony and panicked when I bled into my eyes, causing them to burn and making me unable to see. I rolled over to my side and used my shirt to wipe the blood out of my eyes. I was able to gain my eyesight back to watch Jill take black zip-ties out of her purse.

The helplessness was replaced with rage as I reconciled that death was better than being a victim. I was about to lunge at her until I saw this inconceivable kidnapping and rape become stranger. She put the zip-ties around her wrist and tightened them by pulling the plastic strap with her teeth, shackling herself.

Not wasting the opportunity, I pushed myself off the soiled and bloodied carpet and flew toward her with one leap. I tackled her into the wall and began wrestling for the gun. Her adrenaline kicked in, and she kept a secure grip on the revolver. She kneed me in my raw cock, and I screamed in agony, but I refused to stop wrestling for the gun.

Bang! Bang! Bang! Three shots went off in both our hands as one of us pulled the trigger. Three more shots and the gun would be empty. I reached my finger for the trigger and pulled feverously. Three more deafening shots sounded, followed by the clicks of the firing pin hitting spent shells. She threw the gun at me as I pushed her off me, but she missed. I was ready to throw my weight into punching her until I saw her run for the door. I gave chase as we ran through the decrepit dealership. We were nearly out the door when I saw the blue and red flashing lights coming to us. I slowed down and felt the sweet relief of rescue began to overtake me. I was finally safe.

"Help me! Help me! He tried to rape me!" Jill screamed.

I came to a complete stop as I tried to register what she just said. Then the realization rushed over me. Both smartphones would have my fingerprints and suggest I discarded them to keep them from being pinpointed by the cell towers and keep her from calling for help. Jill put the child locks on my car doors, the torn panties, and the zip-ties on her wrist would imply I kidnapped. The Viagra so I would be able to keep an erect penis during the painful penetration so there would be DNA in and on her. The gun fired in both of our hands so gunshot residue would be all over us. Jill clawing my face would suggest self-defense. Jill set me up as her rapist.

"He tried to rape me!" she cried as the police pulled up and came to her rescue.

Multiple guns were aimed at me and the police screamed orders at me. I couldn't move, I couldn't register why she would do this to a stranger. I was about to go into shock again until I felt a heavy boot kick me in the back and I fell face-first into the marble floor. The cold metal handcuffs tightened around my wrists, and the world went black.

Three Months Later

I woke up with the heavy lull of depression hanging over me as I rolled out of my hard-twin bed and was welcomed by my dreary gray cell. My trial was tomorrow, but I wasn't optimistic. The police wouldn't believe the inconceivable truth of the events of that hellish night. All of the evidence, the news, and the media were against me. My bloodied mugshot was juxtaposed with her beautiful, evil face and I was labeled a monster by the entire would. Nobody would believe that a 110lbs white women could ever do something as heinous as kidnapping, raping and framing a 210lbs brown man. Even my state-appointed attorney didn't believe me, which was advertised by the expression of disgust he had every time we met to discuss the trial.

Depression hit me hard, and I was placed on suicide watch for a few days. The despair wasn't just from being in prison but from the question which plagued me since that night, why did she do it? This question repeated obsessively in my head for three months and I could never come to a rational answer.

"You've got a visitor," the guard said to me through my cell door slit.

I was escorted to the visitor room and was sat down behind a plexiglass partition, and to my horror, I saw who was sitting on the other side.

"How's prison?" Jill asked.

I was filled with rage and imagined myself breaking through the window and strangling her skinny neck. It would take me one quick twist to break it and I didn't care if I got the death penalty for it, I just wanted her to die by my hands.

A surge of questions went through me, but only one will suffice, the one that plagued me since that night.

"Why?"

Jill paused for a moment and entertained the answer. She looked around to make sure nobody was listening and leaned close to the vents in the glass.

"Because I could," she said with a smile on her face.

The Execution

Terre Haute Penitentiary

Terre Haute, Indiana

November 1st, 2016

2330 hours

Prisoner #112263, a.k.a. John Doe was set to be executed at midnight. You wouldn't think he was capable of killing upon first meeting him. He was a handsome middle-aged man, but he was handsome in the old ways: jet black hair with an aged babyface, a beauty mark on his lip, and a lean body. You would think he was the resurrected Elvis, the Sun Records one when you first laid eyes on him. The guards found his sincerity and quietness disarming; they even came to like the guy until they were reminded of his crime.

His very existence was shrouded with conspiracy theories because he had no identity before April 30th, 2014. The F.B.I., C.I.A., and some men in suits who only said they worked for the government were perplexed by this mystery. No fingerprint records, no school records, not even a social media photo could be found of John Doe before his arrest.

He refused to give his name only admitting to his crime and pleading guilty in court. John Doe didn't even decry the judge for giving him the death penalty.

I was sent by my temple to give John Doe his last rites before his execution. One of the few details the man has given of himself was that he was Jewish. I couldn't say I was too happy with the assignment given the nature of his crime, but my curiosity and the excitement of possibly knowing his true motive superseded my disgust for the man. Too bad I can't tell another soul if he did confess to me.

The guard walked me down the cold and quiet green mile to a foldable aluminum chair in front of a cell. An inmate walked past me pushing a cart with what was left of John Doe's last meal. He must not have been a practicing Jew because there was some leftover bacon on the plate. As the inmate walked past me, I was given my first glimpse of the murderer and was taken aback by his looks. He did look like a young Elvis with a beauty mark, but an Elvis aged heavily by guilt. He was reading the Torah and praying silently, asking for forgiveness from God. Maybe God will forgive him, but I doubt it.

He didn't acknowledge me at first, so I gave the plexiglass a few rattles with my knuckles to get his attention. He slowly looked up, and there was a small smile of relief on his face. I sat down on the chair, adjusted my kippah and pulled out my Torah. Before I could give my name, John Doe asked the question which haunts me in my sleep. The question that has become a cliché but now is a curse to me.

"Rabbi, if you could go back in time to kill Hitler would you do it?" John Doe asked with an uneasy gaze.

My first thought was that the man was insane for that being the first thing he asked me, and I felt like I knew where this was going and I wasn't going to play his game.

"Mr. Doe, I am going to be blunt by not giving in to your delusional question. I'm here to help you make peace with God. Now let's get started..."

"Rabbi, I only ask you to entertain my question because it will aid in my full confession. I know I disgust you; I disgust myself for what I had to do. But, please bear with me so I can finally speak the truth to you before I die."

I hesitated for a moment to entertain an insane murderer, but I wanted to know the truth; to see the mystery behind John Doe.

I exhaled deeply. "It's wrong to kill a person. God forbids it in the commandments, but he also allows for justice too. My grandfather was a Polish Jew during Hitler's reign and the only member of my family to survive Auschwitz..." I took in a long deep sigh as I remembered the stories my Bubbe told me when I was old enough to understand the horrors of the Holocaust.

"I don't know what I would do. Do I break God's law to stop the Holocaust and World War II? Maybe. I never gave thought to such a question because the war and the extermination of our people did happen, and we can't change it. That's my answer. What does this have to do with you murdering Ron Boon?"

John Doe looked down at my feet for a few moments and took a deep breath. "When I was first asked that question, I was positive I would do it without thinking twice. I would walk up to Hitler and blow the monster's brains out and prevent millions of people from dying. I never knew how wrong it feels until I did it."

A tear trickled down John Doe's cheek, but he regained his composure.

"I know how insane my confession will sound. I know you won't believe me; I wouldn't believe it if I heard it, but please hear me out. Listen to it, and I can give you undeniable proof of it at the end."

I sat back in the chair while laying the Torah on my lap and prepared myself for his insane confession.

"My name is Isaac David. I am 44 years old. I was born in Chicago, raised in Wrigleyville, and my birthdate is October 31st, 2000."

I stood up to walk away until he said, "God demands you to hear my confession, no matter how mad it seems."

I was reluctantly reminded of my sacred duty to serve God in any and all capacity, even if I didn't understand it. "Continue," I said in frustration.

"I was raised in Chicago and grew up worshipping the Cubs and physics. On my wall hung posters of Ben Zobrist and Stephen Hawking, an odd combination. Thankfully I was offered both a baseball and an academic scholarship to MIT in 2018, sadly on the same day Hawking died. I felt like it was a glorious sign from the universe at first, but now I know it was an omen of what was to come for me.

I graduated with a Ph.D. in Theoretical Physics in 2024 and was offered jobs with DARPA, Space X, and NASA. But it was CERN I was gunning for, and it took me three separate applications to finally get accepted.

There was turmoil already brewing in Washington by the time I moved to Geneva. A young industrialist named Ron Boon who made his fortune off of cryptocurrency and real estate was gunning for the White House. He was born around the same time I was, and he wasn't legal yet to run for President, but his charisma and his hostile rhetoric were winning support from the voters who felt disenfranchised and undermined by the politicians in office. The U.S. was no longer a world power in 2024 due to the endless war in the middle east and democracy being hollowed out and replaced with cowardly but powerful politicians controlled by an oligarchical mess of greedy industrialists. Greed had mutilated true capitalism, and the land of democracy was no longer home of the free. I was happy to leave.

Ron Boon was a man of pure Id, but he was sincere, which was refreshing compared to the marionettes called Congress. I was in the airport waiting for my flight to Geneva when I saw Ron Boon giving a speech on the steps of Congress. His aggressive and expressive hand gestures, his talks of nationalism and his blame on immigrants seemed familiar to me. I couldn't...I wouldn't assume at the time, but now I know that I had watched the genesis of America's Hitler.

I was glad to have left the U.S. and I lived in a scientist's paradise. I was surrounded by openminded and rational people in a beautiful country where science and rational thought was celebrated and not shunned for the facts it uncovered. But, most of all I was working on a classified project funded by the EU, Bill Gates, and Elon Musk. The project was to see if we could use the particle accelerator to manipulate space and time. It took us 15 years of research and experimentation, but we had finally found a way to travel through time."

Mr. John Doe or Isaac David, whatever his name was, had me hooked. Not because I believed him, which I didn't, but it was a good story he was spinning. "Ok, I'll bite. How did you break the laws of physics and God?" I asked.

Isaac had a small smile of excitement until he realized I was humoring him and I still didn't believe him. "I'm going to use an analogy so you can understand. Imagine our dimension as an entire river. Space/Matter is the water in the river. Water because matter transforms into different states and it is always changing. The stream bed is time because time is what moves space and matter forward and changes it. Time is the barrier, the control, the constant."

"Uhh, time is not always constant. I know a little bit of physics, and I know time can be bent. Our famous Jewish physicist proved this."

Isaac smiled in delight which made me unconsciously smile.

"Yes, Rabbi. You are correct. Gravity can warp time. Keeping with the analogy, if the stream of water is space/matter and the stream bed is time, then gravity would be some variation. Depending on how dense the gravitational field is, then it could be a simple boulder in the river which slightly interrupts a stream, a dam which controls the flow of the river, or a canal which connects the river to another river or another body of water."

"You have my curiosity but how's this bullshit supposed to help you time travel?"

"The sun has a dense enough mass to bend the path of light. The sun is a boulder. A Black Hole is like a dam because it completely interrupts space/matter. We used gravity to create a canal, a wormhole, through space and time.

"The first time we sent a quark two seconds in the future and found it unchanged. Then we received a molecule in our vacuum chamber out of nowhere. After 5 minutes we cleared the chamber and added an identical molecule and made it disappear. It never reappeared until we realized that the molecule we initially received was the one we thought we sent forward, but it went back into time. We had sent something infinitely larger than a quark into the past. We had earned our place with Newton, Einstein, and Hawking.

This was in 2040, and the world was on the brink of another World War. President Ron Boon had taken office young and declared himself, with the blind loyalty of his party, the U.S.'s first Caesar a.k.a. Dictator. It was slow at first. He chipped away at people's privacy and rights, took control of competing businesses, and blamed the sorrows of America on immigrants, gays, Muslims, the news, and anyone else who opposed him.

He sent troops into Mexico and Central America and annexed their countries. England and Australia supported him, but the rest of the world was prepping for an all-out war against the U.S.

I had moved my family out of the U.S. and into France. The Americans who were intelligent enough to understand history saw it repeating itself and fled to Canada, South America, and Asia. The rest were blinded by the evil of President Boon, or they couldn't afford to leave. A national draft was established where every young man and woman had to either join the military, work for the war factories, or go to the concentration camps where they kept the POW's, immigrants, and dissenters." Isaac stopped as he turned his head in an attempt to hide his tears.

"September 7th, 2041 is the day the world ended. The fucking greedy bastard nuked Ottawa because Canada was the only one country willing to oppose the U.S. The Canadians never had nuclear weapons, but they had made a secret pact with the E.U., Russia, and China. The E.U. agreed with the pact for honorable reasons, but China and Russia wanted to take their competitor out of the picture. Russia and China aimed their nukes at the U.S. and ordered the President to surrender. But Boon never cared what was best for his people, and he acted out of hate and impulse. He ordered preeminent strikes on Moscow, Beijing, and Paris.

"Immediately there was a mutiny among the military with most of the Generals and Admirals refusing the order, and they went to arrest President Boon. But a few sons of bitches blinded by their patriotism and stupidity followed the order and shot nukes at Paris and Moscow. Moscow was able to shoot down most of the nukes, but they missed one, and the Kremlin was gone. Paris was turned to radioactive ash. England and Australia shot their nuke, and mutually assured destruction was actualized.

"Hell was created that day. Fire and brimstone rained from the heavens and turned the Earth into ash. There was weeping and gnashing of teeth for anyone who survived. The sun was blotted out by the nuclear clouds and what was left of the world was slowly dying on a planet called Hell.

"Switzerland was the least damaged, but that's like saying that a certain tree had some bark left after the forest was incinerated. Fortunately, we had a plan. In 2042, what space program was left of humanity sent survivors to Mars and the Moon for the continuity of our species.

"The greatest scientist and engineers left on this world worked underground for nearly two years. We split into teams who built, calculated, and reimagined new technology and equations that bordered on the supernatural. The will of man can rival God if motivated enough. By 2044, most of us were dying from starvation or radiation sickness, but we succeeded in creating a time machine.

"It was a sphere built large enough for one person. The shell was made of an intelligent alloy which adapts and changes to extreme pressure and temperatures. It was reversed engineered from the cephalopod's ability to change its body composition, skin texture and heal itself. The sphere was only a life raft and had no propulsion. The collider had enough power to fling the sphere to what we estimated to be 2025— enough time to assassinate President Ron Boon before he gained power.

"I was asked to be the one to go back in the past because I was American, and it was my great discovery that would save humanity. The downside was that this trip was one-shot, one-way. One-shot because the gravity needed to send the sphere back was going to destroy the facility and possibly the Eastern Hemisphere. One-way because... well.

"Rabbi, you have to understand how desperate we were. Not only was humanity being extinguished from Earth, but the planet may never be home to life again. The environment will never be hospitable even to the most resilient microbe which would've evolved to become the next dominant species. We had our miracle of science, and we needed to save not only mankind but life itself.

"I was given gold bullion to trade for cash when I arrived in 2025, in addition to an antique smartphone to help me on my dire quest. The last thing was a 20-year-old Glock from a former NASA scientist and Naval Pilot; he asked me to save the American dream before it became the world's nightmare.

"We tearfully said our goodbyes and the scientists, engineers, and physicists who survived the apocalypse made peace before they gave their lives to send me back into time. Strapped into the spherical raft with a viewscreen taking the place of a porthole, I watched as they bravely switched on the collider and prepared to die. A deafening and violent sound of thunder followed by a strange sense of weightlessness caused me overwhelming fear until the raft suddenly accelerated to a few G-Forces. I forced myself to stay conscious as I looked through the viewfinder and saw..."

Isaac lunged forward from his cell's bed and threw up violently into the toilet. If this was all an act, then it was the best fucking acting I've ever seen. He sat down next to the toilet, exhausted from the vomiting and continued his fantastic story.

"Using the analogy about our reality being a river and the wormhole acting as the canal to an earlier part of the river, then what I saw was the dark and terrifying forest surrounding the river, and it was insanity. The laws of physics were no longer applicable as I saw fiery planets floating on oceans of black mold. I couldn't make sense of the objects I was looking at nor could I tell if they were creatures, but they were the size of mountains and they were looking at me. I cried for God and wished to go back to the apocalyptic world I left because it was far less terrifying then what I was seeing.

"One of the large Lovecraftian creatures reached out for me with its oscillating spindle claw, and I screamed as I took the Glock and put it against my head. The raft was then flushed with bright light, and I felt weightless and peaceful as I saw through the viewscreen for a brief moment of what I can only describe as the symmetry of existence. For a brief moment, I saw the multi-verse and the micro-verse in its entirety.

"The next thing I know I crashed hard onto the solid ground and the sphere-raft rolled for a while until it stopped. The viewfinder showed the light from the sun, trees, and ironically, a river. I crawled out of the hatch and cried in happiness as I felt the luscious green grass, the cold forest air, and washed my face in the clear stream. I selfishly spent the night in the forest basking in the warmth of a small campfire I made. I wanted to enjoy Earth again before the war.

"That morning I hesitantly turned on the antique phone and waited for a signal and the GPS to come on. The phone picked up a signal and started to boot up. I had landed somewhere outside Roanoke, Virginia but I shrieked in horror when I saw the date. It was February 11th, 2014. At first, I thought it was a good thing that I was given an extra ten years to complete the mission, but then I realized the monster I was sent to kill wasn't a grown man but a boy.

"I set the raft to self-destruct to make sure the technology couldn't be used before it's time and hiked my way to Roanoke. I found a gold dealer in town and traded some of the gold bullion for cash. I bought a used gasoline-powered

4Runner and drove with a vengeful determination to Georgetown where Google told me the monster lived with his wealthy family.

"The closer I got the more my anger subsided and gave way to doubt as I realize I was about to shoot a boy and not the monster he would become. I glanced at the Glock handle protruding from the open rucksack and was immediately reminded of how he destroyed all of life for his fucking ego.

"It was dusk when I arrived in Prospect St., outside of his family's colonial mansion. The rage got me ready to pull the trigger as I imagined me easily walking up to him and emptying the magazine into his head. He's guilty no matter how much my consciousness reminded me he was just a child.

"Then I saw the child Ron Boon, innocently walking home by himself while carrying his baseball equipment. I realized we're the same age and if we met when we were young, then we may have bonded over baseball. The rage started to fade as an immense shame and fear replaced it. The Glock trembled in my hand, and I couldn't force myself to get out of the car and kill the boy who would become the devourer of worlds.

"He walked inside his house, and I sat in the 4Runner for hours and cried. I was tormented by this simple decision. What difference does it make if he is a boy or a man, he is still going to destroy the world? I forced myself to drive and found a hotel nearby where I didn't leave the room for a week as I tried to rectify the dilemma for myself.

"Is this boy responsible for the decisions he will make in the future? Can he be changed, maybe influenced not to become the world's last dictator? Can existence risk him continuing to breathe? Should this boy die to save Earth? One soul for the entire planet. Is it his fate to become the destroyer of worlds?

"These existential questions plagued me for that god-awful week as I fell sick from the heavy burden. The solution I came to was to stalk him. I had time to do it and may be gathering more information about Ron would guide me on if killing him is the best choice.

"I rented an apartment close by and spent nearly two months watching the boy and his family. The father was a greedy bastard who committed treason just for a good deal. His mother was indifferent as long as she was fed expensive wine from Spain and Oxycontin. But, Ron himself seemed well-adjusted. He had friends, played sports and even had a part-time job working at his father's firm.

"I began to admire this boy and nearly stopped comparing him to his older self until that fateful sunny April weekend. I always kept my distance and never came within 50 yards of Ron, but I needed a closer look. There was a national park nearby where he would go hiking, but I never followed him because I didn't want my cover to be blown. I found myself trekking after him with the Glock hidden underneath my jacket. His hike seemed unremarkable, but I kept my 50-yard distance until I lost sight of him. I spent a few minutes trying to find him until I heard muffled squeals coming from an overhang near me.

"I approached quietly to the edge of the overhang and witnessed the gruesome truth. Ron Boon was standing over a sleeping homeless man, and he was pouring his canteen onto the man. The bum was too drunk to notice the smell, but the stench of kerosene stung my nostrils. Ron lit a match, smiled and flicked it onto the homeless man.

"The man woke up screaming and began rolling in the dirt and leaves but that only spread the fire across his body. I found myself paralyzed by the shock of the gruesome act as I watched in horror as Ron laughed as the man cried for help and tried fruitlessly to pull off the layers of flaming clothes which were charring his flesh. Ron's hideous laughter stopped when he looked up and saw me.

"We stared into each other's eyes and at that moment I knew that fucking kid needed to die. I reached into my pocket for the Glock, but he began to run. I stumbled and fell over the overhang, landing next to the dying homeless man. I stared into the dying man's eyes and saw every life Ron Boon had killed looking back at me. I picked myself up and ran after him. He was 40 yards ahead of me as we ran toward the mouth of the trail. I was picking up speed and getting closer to him until he ran into a public area and began to scream for help.

"Ron got the attention of a few parkgoers and a Park Ranger. I stopped and tried to hide, but he pointed at me saying I killed a homeless man and I was trying to kill him. A few people saw my face and the Ranger reached for his gun.

"Time slowed down, and I had a clear shot at Ron, but I would have risked hitting the Ranger and a family downrange of Ron. I instead fired one shot in the air, which caused everyone to run and the Ranger to take cover. The chaos bought me time to run back into the woods and look for a way out.

"It took me an hour of running, but I was able to escape the park and made it back to the apartment unnoticed. I put on the news and watched as Ron Boon pinned the homeless man's murder on me. There was a manhunt for a person of my description, but thankfully there were no photos of me. I grabbed whatever I brought with me from the future and abandoned my apartment and drove to Maryland.

"I spent two weeks hiding in a motel, waiting for the manhunt to dissipate. I dyed my hair and grew a beard to disguise myself and went back to check out the Boon family house. Nobody noticed me, but the family had hired private security to watch their home and follow them anywhere they went. My heart raced as I tried to come up with a solution, one place where I could trap him and get him by surprise. In killing a monster, I was going to become one.

"On April 30th, 2014, I had destroyed anything that would identify who I was and prepared myself for the atrocity I was going to commit. I prayed to God for another way, but I knew deep down that there was no other. I waited in the tree line outside Ron's school and waited for him to go to class. The two ex-military guys sat outside in their blacked-out SUV, but there were no security guards patrolling the school. I prayed to God to help me find another way and if there wasn't then let me complete my mission. I hated myself and cried for what I was about to do, but it needed to be done.

"I saw Ron sitting next to the window of his classroom and knew I had him trapped. I snuck into the back entrance and walked quickly down the empty school hallways, every step closer to the classroom made my heartbeat loud enough to cause a painful humming in my ears. Tears were flowing down my cheeks when I swung that classroom door open. All eyes were upon me. The teacher stopped her lesson and froze in shock. Ron and I met eyes, and I hesitated for a moment.

"But my hand didn't as I raised the gun at him and unloaded the magazine into him.

"The screaming...the screaming. I can still hear the kids screaming as they ran out behind me. I fell to my knees with just me and the corpse of the child Ron Boon, who would never become the apocalypse.

"I brought the gun to my head and kept pulling the trigger in the hope there was one bullet left because I couldn't live with what I just did. I killed a kid. I heard the door fling open behind me followed by multiple expletives and orders from Ron's bodyguards for me to drop the gun and get on the ground. I wanted them to shoot me and was about to swing my gun around to them so they would be forced to, but I felt a hard boot in my back and fell hard onto the linoleum floor. They jumped on top of me and restrained me.

"I kept screaming, begging them to shoot me but they didn't want me to take the easy way out.

"I refused to give away my identity and the reason why I killed Ron Boon. I was interrogated by every U.S. agency with an acronym. They had no fingerprints, no DNA and no one from the public could identify me because I was never arrested or had my fingerprints taken when I was a kid.

"The circus of a trial brought out every conspiracy theorist nut in the world trying to figure out why a man with no identity would kill a child in school. A few of the crazy ones got it right, but who would believe them?

"I offered no defense and accepted the guilty verdict. The Judge had a constant look of disgust on his face throughout the trial, and only smiled when he sentenced me to death. I gladly accepted because I couldn't live with the guilt of killing a child, even if he were to become the harbinger of the apocalypse.

"Now we're here, Rabbi."

I was dumbfounded by his story. I started just entertaining this man with his cry for help, and now I found myself believing him. Was it true, did he save the world and stop the apocalypse? Or was it a mad man's delusional attempt to justify himself for killing a child in school?

The clock struck 12, and the heavy march of boots was heard from a distance. The guards were coming to take Isaac to his execution. I snapped myself out of the rabbit hole of thought and confusion and remembered what Isaac said in the beginning.

"You offered me undeniable proof of your story, tell me now before they take you away."

The march of boots echoed faster and harder, and Isaac motioned me to lean in which I immediately did.

"On November 7th, the Chicago Cubs will win the World Series in Game 7; ending their 108-year drought. They will win in an extra-inning, there will be a rain delay which will work to the Cubs advantage, and the final score will be 8-7. Zobrist will be awarded the World Series MVP. That was one part of history I wished to relive. Too bad I will never see it, again."

The guards walked past me as I sat dumbfounded in my seat with my Torah falling to the ground. Is this man a saint or a monster? Was his incredible story true or a complete utter fabrication from a man wracked from guilt from killing a boy?

John Doe, or Isaac David, made his bed in the cell and then thanked the two guards for how they treated him during his incarceration. The guards tried to keep stoic expressions on their faces, but a single tear from each betrayed their true feelings about the man they were about to execute.

Another guard retrieved me from my stupor, and I was escorted into the chamber where they strapped Isaac down to a gurney in the shape of a cross. I gave him his final rites and held his hand for a moment. His final words to me were, "Did I do the right thing?"

I couldn't breathe at that moment. I wanted to believe him. I desperately wanted to believe John Doe was really Isaac David and his incredible story was true, but I couldn't. I said nothing but cried as he was injected with the poison, and he went into a deep quiet sleep and then died.

November 3rd, 2016

Chicago, Illinois

I made a few calls the day after John Doe/Isaac David was executed and found a boy named Isaac David who attends a synagogue in Chicago. I thought about seeing the boy for myself to see if he was the younger version of John Doe, but I dismissed the idea because it was crazy. Am I going to believe a man traveled back in time to stop the nuclear apocalypse? If I did, then I would be as mad as John Doe was.

But last night the Cubs won the World Series. The first time in over 108 years. And they won exactly like Isaac David said they would. I sat in front of my T.V. and began to cry tears of sadness and gratefulness. I've met a man who saved the world, and I didn't believe him. I got in my car and drove all night to Chicago to go to the synagogue the young Isaac David attended.

The Rabbi knew the David family well and said the boy was a genius and an athlete, even going as far as calling him the next Einstein. He told me that the boy was playing in the park next to the synagogue because schools were closed for the Cubs victory.

My heart raced in anticipation as I walked across the street and saw the neighborhood kids playing baseball in the park. But then I saw him. Like a teen Elvis with a birthmark on his lip, Isaac David slammed a home run out of the park, and everybody cheered, calling him the Jewish Zobrist.

Isaac caught me staring with a wide smile on my face and came running to me.

"Hello, Rabbi. Did you see how far I hit that ball? I must have sent it into Lake Michigan," he said with exuberance.

"That you did, my son. That you did," were the only words I found myself saying to him.

He started to walk away until I called him back.

"Yes, Rabbi," he said with a bright smile.

"I wanted to let you know that you are and will always be a good man and the world is a better place because of you."

He smiled awkwardly at the compliment but sincerely thanked me for it. He ran back to the game and his friends as I found a park bench and watched the children play a game of baseball.

Made in the USA
Columbia, SC
09 September 2020